BOOKS BY
RACHELLE DELANEY

Clara Voyant

The Bonaventure Adventures

The Metro Dogs of Moscow
The Circus Dogs of Prague

The Ship of Lost Souls
The Lost Souls of Island X
The Hunt for the Panther

ALICE FLECK'S RECIPES FOR
DISASTER

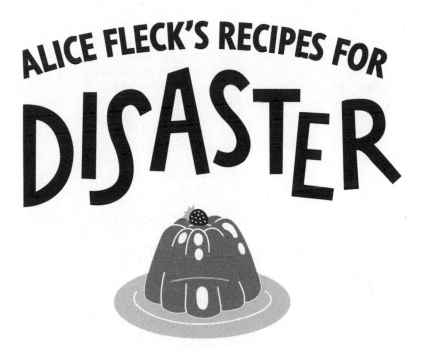

RACHELLE DELANEY

Puffin Canada, an imprint of Penguin Random House Canada Young
Readers, a division of Penguin Random House of Canada Limited

Library and Archives Canada Cataloguing in Publication

Title: Alice Fleck's recipes for disaster / Rachelle Delaney.
Other titles: Recipes for disaster
Names: Delaney, Rachelle, author.
Identifiers: Canadiana (print) 20200211412 | Canadiana (ebook) 20200211420
| ISBN 9780735269279 (hardcover) | ISBN 9780735269286 (EPUB)
Classification: LCC PS8607.E48254 A79 2021 | DDC jC813/.6 — dc23

Library of Congress Control Number: 2020936741

Edited by Lynne Missen
Designed by Emma Dolan
The text was set in Albertina.

Printed and bound in Canada

www.penguinrandomhouse.ca

1 2 3 4 5   25 24 23 22 21

Penguin
Random House
PUFFIN CANADA

For Eric

CHAPTER

1

O n her very last day of elementary school, Alice Fleck arrived home to find an unexpected gift.

"Open it!" Her father pressed a rectangular box into her hands as she dropped her backpack near the door. James Fleck's gray eyes were bright and his ginger hair bedheaded despite his best attempts to tame it.

She lifted the lid and gasped. "A *phone*? You're kidding!" She held it up in awe.

"Congratulations on finishing sixth grade!" James beamed. "I'm proud of you, sous-chef."

"But . . . but . . ." She stared at the shiny black cell phone in her hand as if it might suddenly disappear. "What about the kaleidoscopes?"

According to Alice's father, some young people in the nineteenth century had been completely and utterly obsessed with kaleidoscopes. They carried them everywhere they went, and sometimes ended up bumping into trees or walking into horse-drawn carriages with their kaleidoscopes pressed to their eyes. James maintained that this was a true story, an important piece of history, though Alice found it hard to believe. He also maintained

1

that cell phones were like the kaleidoscopes of the twenty-first century: a menace to society.

"I stand by my theory," he told her. "But you're starting middle school soon, and I heard somewhere that cell phones are a necessity in middle school." He raised a ginger eyebrow at her.

She shrugged innocently. "I wonder where you heard that." She'd only mentioned it a few hundred times over the past year.

"I can't imagine. Anyway, it's a time of big changes for us, so it seemed like the time for this too."

Alice didn't like the sound of big changes, but she did like the feeling of the phone in her hand. She gave him a huge hug.

"It's secondhand," he added, sounding apologetic. "It belonged to Hana — she was getting a new one. But it's in very good condition. You know Hana."

Alice felt her smile fade. She stepped back, mumbling that she didn't really know Hana at all. But he didn't seem to hear.

You got a phone, she reminded herself. *Who cares who it came from?* Gone were the days of being the only kid who couldn't send text messages or squeal over a new suite of emojis. It was as if she'd just stepped into the modern era.

She began to ask if she could run across the street to show her friend Mat, but a knock at the door interrupted her.

James smoothed his shirt, which he'd ironed that morning but now looked as though he'd slept in it. "That must be Hana now!"

"Now?"

"I invited her for dinner. Did I not mention that?"

Alice shook her head — he most definitely had not. She'd been hoping they could spend the evening by themselves, maybe catching up on their favorite cooking show, *Culinary Chronicles,* or trying out a new recipe. They'd recently found one for a croquembouche that appealed to them both. James was excited by its history; the croquembouche was traditionally served at French weddings. Alice was excited to try building a cone-shaped tower of cream puffs bound together with threads of spun sugar.

But now James was flinging open the door and exclaiming "Hana!" as if he hadn't seen her for months when it had probably been only a few hours. So Alice had no choice but to bid her plans for the evening goodbye and steel herself to greet Hana Holmes.

Her father's new girlfriend.

Hana and James had met at the university, where they both worked in the Department of History. James was a culinary historian, which meant he studied the history of food. Culinary historians could also be called food historians, but James preferred "culinary historian" for the same reason he liked to call his and Alice's hair "ginger" instead of "orange." It just had a nicer ring to it.

Hana studied the Victorian era, the period from 1837 to 1901, so called because Queen Victoria had ruled over Great Britain back then. She'd explained this to Alice the first time they'd met, back in April. And Alice, who'd just learned that her father had been dating Hana since *February* but hadn't bothered to tell Alice, had informed Hana that she knew what the Victorian era was, thank you very much.

Hana had been making regular appearances at inopportune times ever since.

She bounced through the front door, smiling as usual, and cried "Alice!" as if seeing her was the most exciting part of her day.

Alice forced a smile that she hoped looked genuine but not *too* friendly.

Hana Holmes looked nothing like any historian Alice had ever met. Most of her father's colleagues dressed in tweed and corduroy and were usually in need of a haircut. Hana wore jeans and T-shirts, often paired with matching nail polish (today, a candy-apple red). She had straight and shiny black hair and bangs that grazed her eyebrows so perfectly Alice suspected she must trim them every day. It made her even more aware of her own hair, which, like her father's, was utterly untamable. She pulled it into a braid each morning, but by lunchtime it was all frizz and flyaways.

"Hana's pretty cool," Alice's friend Mat Diaz had recently observed. They'd been sitting on Mat's front step across the street, watching Hana park her sporty black car outside the Flecks' townhouse.

Alice had frowned. "How do you know?"

He shrugged. "Cami said so. She said Hana's about as cool as an adult can be."

Mat's fifteen-year-old sister Cami was an authority on such things, so Alice couldn't very well argue. But it didn't change her opinion of her father's new girlfriend. Hana Holmes was *unnecessary*. Alice and James had been perfectly happy without her.

Still, she thanked Hana for the phone. That was only polite.

"You're very welcome." Hana gave her a toothy smile. "And I have something else for you!" She dug into her tote bag and pulled out a box the color of pistachio ice cream. The name Ladurée was printed on the top in gold script.

Alice lifted the lid, uncovering a row of dainty sandwich cookies, each a different color of the rainbow. "Macarons!" she gasped, forgetting to hide her excitement. She and her father had once spent a weekend trying to perfect the confections, which were as tricky to make as they were delicious: the cookies were made of almond meringue, sandwiched together with buttercream or ganache. According to James, macarons had been invented by Venetian monks in the eighth century. Back then, they were called "priests' bellybuttons."

She felt like she'd been given a box of rare jewels. "Thank you," she said again, wishing Hana weren't quite so good with gifts.

"We'll have them for dessert!" James proclaimed. "What a treat."

Alice nodded, carefully closing the lid. "So what's for dinner?"

"Good question." He ushered them down the hall and into the kitchen, where he picked up a cookbook from the counter: *Magnificent Medieval Meals (Volume 12)*. "I saw a recipe for mutton stew that looked interesting."

"Hana's vegetarian," Alice reminded him.

"Yes, of course." He slammed the book shut. "I knew that."

"How about pizza?" she suggested.

"Excellent idea!" he cried. "I have a recipe somewhere for the very first pizza ever made. Archaeologists found remains of it from seven thousand years ago!"

"Did they?" Hana marveled.

Alice could only guess what kinds of toppings the archaeologists had found on a seven-thousand-year-old pizza. "How about takeout?" She held up her new phone. "I'll call."

Once the pizza had been ordered, she turned back to James. "Can I go to Mat's to show him my phone? I'll be back before the pizza gets here."

5

"Sure," he said. "But first, let's hear Hana's news."

"Hmm?" Hana looked up from an ancient Roman spork she'd been inspecting — one of several very old kitchen tools they had lying around the house, and one of Alice's favorites, because who needed a spoon *and* a fork when you could have both together?

"You told me on the phone that you had news for us." He sat down at the kitchen table and gestured for them to join him. Alice stayed standing, hoping it wouldn't take long.

"Oh, yes." Hana smiled again, but this time her lips quivered ever so slightly.

Was Hana nervous? Alice wondered, watching her fiddle with the Roman spork. Maybe her news was bad. *Maybe* she was about to tell them that she'd gotten a job in another city and had to move away. Alice pulled up a chair to listen.

Hana drew a breath. "It's exciting news. I hope you'll like it." She gave James an anxious look, and he nodded encouragingly.

Alice hoped he wouldn't be too disappointed.

"You know the Victorian festival we've been talking about?"

"Yes, of course," said James.

"Victorian festival?" said Alice.

"Hana will be lecturing at a Victorian festival in a few weeks," James explained. "It's a week-long event at an old manor in the country, where people will learn all about Victorian times. I've been thinking we should go with her. Sounds fun, right?"

Fun wasn't how Alice would have described a week-long Victorian festival, especially one James and Hana had been planning to attend without telling her. "Not really, no."

He ignored this. "So, what's the news?"

"Well . . ." Hana drummed her candy-apple fingernails on the table. "Remember when you two cooked that medieval peacock pie?"

James tsked. "Once again, I'm so sorry you couldn't try it."

"You didn't miss much," Alice told her. The meat had been as tough as leather, and James had insisted on adding so many spices that they'd had to gulp down water between bites.

"Right." Hana bit her lip. "And . . . remember how I took that video of you two making the pie?"

Alice nodded, recalling how Hana had whipped out her phone to capture the action, and Alice had cringed down to her toes. The last thing she wanted was for anyone to see her making peacock pie.

"You were just so delightful to watch," Hana went on. "A father and daughter culinary history duo — I'd never seen anything like it! And James, you told that great story about the spice trade and that . . . that cinnamon bird!"

Alice nodded again — she loved that story too. But she had no idea where Hana was going with this, and it was making her nervous.

A terrible thought came to mind: what if Hana had posted the video online, and it had gone viral? What if people around the world were laughing at them, wondering what kind of weirdos spent a Friday night cooking a peacock pie? And who would kill such a beautiful bird? Alice still wasn't sure about that — her father had ordered the peacock online, and it been delivered to their doorstep, already plucked like a grocery store chicken.

She gripped the table, readying herself for the worst.

"You're going to be on *Culinary Chronicles!*" Hana blurted.

They blinked at her.

"I'm sorry, what?" said James.

"The TV show?" said Alice.

Hana gulped and nodded.

"Um . . ." James looked at Alice, then back at Hana. "I don't understand."

"Okay." She pressed her palms together. "I'll explain. About a month ago, I found out that *Culinary Chronicles* was being filmed at this Victorian festival. I know you two love the show, and I thought you'd be perfect contestants. I also knew you'd be free to go, since we'd talked about going to the festival together. Right?" She looked at James.

"Er, yes," he said.

Alice glanced between them, wondering how many other things they'd planned without telling her. But she stayed quiet, still deeply confused.

"So I sent the show's producers that video. And they loved you! I heard back from them this morning. You're in, both of you: James will be the lead cook, and Alice the assistant. Isn't that great?"

James's mouth fell open. "Hana . . ."

"I know I should have asked you first!" she hurried on. "But you wouldn't have put together an application — I know how much you hate paperwork!" She laughed. "And I think this could be really good for you." She grabbed his hand and squeezed it.

Normally their hand-holding made Alice squirm, but now she had bigger things to worry about. "Hang on a minute," she said, trying to keep her voice even. "Let me get this straight. We're going to be on *Culinary Chronicles*, which is being filmed in a few weeks at a *Victorian festival*?"

"Uh-huh," said Hana. "Apparently this season is all about Victorian food. I guess every season's different?"

Alice nodded. Every season on *Culinary Chronicles,* a new group of amateur cooks gathered to recreate dishes from a particular time in history. She and James had seen every episode — he loved it when the host delved into little-known parts of culinary history, like the bakeries of ancient Pompeii or the evolution of the nutmeg grater. Alice liked watching the contestants race against the clock to create interesting dishes.

But she'd never wanted to be on the show. Not even a little bit.

"So, what do you think?" Hana asked in a small voice.

"I think . . ." James hesitated, then squeezed her hand back. "I think it's amazing news. What a surprise. Right, Alice? Isn't it an exciting surprise?"

"It's a surprise all right," said Alice.

"Oh, I'm so glad," Hana cried. "For a moment there I was worried you wouldn't like it."

"Of course we do," James assured her.

She turned to Alice. "Can you imagine what the kids at your new middle school will say when they find out one of their classmates is on *Culinary Chronicles?*"

Alice opened her mouth, then shut it. She didn't have to imagine — she knew exactly what the kids at school would say.

Which was why they could never find out.

"This is my favorite episode." James pointed at the screen of his old laptop, where the contestants were attempting to whip eggs into a soufflé.

"You say that about every episode." Alice picked a raspberry-red macaron out of the box and took a bite. It was sweet and tart, crispy and chewy all at once. Perfection.

Hana had left soon after dinner, and James and Alice had retreated to the library to watch *Culinary Chronicles*. It wasn't a real library, of course — just a corner of the living room furnished with stacks of books and two old reading chairs. But they'd called it the library since they'd moved to the townhouse two years earlier. After living in a tiny apartment for ten years, the two-bedroom townhouse felt like a mansion to Alice. And what was a mansion without a library?

"They're all my favorites." James dusted sky-blue macaron crumbs off his shirt. "Ooh, this is where Mei-Ling explains the origins of the soufflé!" He leaned forward and propped his elbows on his knees.

Alice finished off her macaron. She felt better now that Hana had left but still unsettled by her news. She and her father would be competing on *Culinary Chronicles*. She tried to imagine it but couldn't.

"I don't know if I can do it," she said.

"Do what?" James asked.

"This." Alice gestured to the laptop. "I don't know if I can be on *Culinary Chronicles*." She swallowed. "I don't want to be on TV."

He turned to her. "I know, sous-chef. I've never wanted to be on TV either. But maybe it'll be fun — it *is* a pretty friendly show." He looked back at the screen: one of the competitors was lamenting a deflated soufflé, and the others had clustered around to console her.

Alice knew this. *Culinary Chronicles* was quite possibly the friendliest cooking competition on TV. The judges were forgiving. The host was kind. The contestants didn't get sent home if they messed up, like they did on other shows. They were even allowed to bring assistants to help them.

Which was precisely why no one watched it — at least according to Mat's sister Cami. She'd explained this to Alice after overhearing her telling Mat about a particularly exciting episode. "It's on the History Alive network," Cami had added with a grimace.

Alice had flushed tomato-red and vowed never to mention the show again.

"Don't forget," said James, "you'd get to meet Mei-Ling."

That made Alice smile. Mei-Ling Wu, the host of *Culinary Chronicles*, was warm and charming — she could make the contestants laugh even in the most stressful situations. Just then, on James's laptop, she was hugging the contestant with the deflated soufflé.

"It would be fun to meet her," Alice admitted.

"Look, sous-chef, it's up to you," said James. "If you don't want to do this, we won't. But I think it could be fun. We've cooked a ton of Victorian dishes together. Remember that time we made fifty-seven pork pies?"

"How could I forget?" James had been writing an article titled "The Surprising History of the Pork Pie" and wanted to make sure he got it right.

"And what's more, we'd be supporting Hana at this festival thing! She's a bit nervous about her lectures, and I think she'd appreciate some friendly faces in the audience."

Alice said nothing to this. Supporting Hana wasn't high on her list of priorities.

James turned to watch the judge sample the soufflés, and Alice tried to imagine what it would be like to compete as her father's assistant — his sous-chef, as he liked to say. Maybe it would feel perfectly natural — she had, after all, been helping him for as long as she could remember. Over the years, they'd recreated more historical dishes than she could count, everything from ancient Egyptian honey candy to Viking porridge and Victorian pork pies.

Knowing they'd be in it together made her feel a bit better.

And if Cami Diaz was right, it was unlikely that any kids would ever see it. It would live quietly on the History Alive network, which no one watched.

With any luck, she could keep it all on the down-low.

"**Y**ou okay, Alice? Sorry it's a bit tight back there."

"A bit tight" was an understatement: Alice barely fit in the backseat of Hana's car, thanks in no small part to Hana's luggage. For the week they'd be spending at Gladstone Manor, where the festival would take place, she'd packed a large suitcase, a duffel bag, a briefcase, a backpack and not one, not two, but *three* umbrellas!

Who needs three umbrellas in July? Alice wondered, setting her feet on a stack of cookbooks. Already her stomach felt pinched. She hoped she wouldn't be sick on the drive.

"Road trip!" Hana sang from the driver's seat.

"I *love* a good road trip," James declared, buckling himself into the seat beside hers.

Alice tried to remember the last time they'd taken one. Their old VW Beetle hadn't been road trip–worthy in years.

She stared out the window at the Diaz house as they pulled away from the curb. The blinds in Mat's bedroom window had been drawn since he'd left for art camp the previous week. She hadn't heard from him since.

Send me pics of your dioramas? she'd texted the day he

left. Mat was obsessed with dioramas and planned to spend his month at camp making them nonstop.

I'll post them on PHOMO, he'd messaged back. You HAVE to get an account now that you have a phone!

Mat had been raving about PHOMO for months. As Alice understood it, it was a pretty simple phone app: you set up an account, then posted photos for others to see and checked out the photos other people posted. Her life, according to Mat, was incomplete without PHOMO.

James disagreed. He couldn't see why Alice needed to look at strangers' photos and share her own.

"I'll only follow Mat," she'd promised. "And maybe an account about dogs in sweaters — Mat says it's amazing. Anyway, I'll keep my own account private."

But James wasn't convinced. "It's just another reason for you to stare at your phone," he'd lamented. "Soon you'll be bumping into trees and walking into horse-drawn carriages."

"You mean, like, cars?" Alice had said, but the conversation was over.

As they left the neighborhood and headed for the highway, she took out her phone to see if Mat had sent a message from camp. He hadn't. She tucked it away again.

According to Hana, it was a three-hour drive to Gladstone Manor, but judging by how fast she was driving Alice assumed they'd get there in considerably less time. She tightened her seatbelt as they merged onto the highway and tried not to peek at the speedometer.

To distract herself, she took a book titled *The Victorian Cooking Compendium* from the stack under her feet, then tapped her father on the shoulder. "Quiz?"

He glanced back. "Already? Oh, okay. Mind if we practice, Hana?"

"Not at all." She turned down the music on her phone.

Alice flipped through the cookbook. They'd been practicing like this for the past two weeks: she would name a dish and, without looking at the recipe, he would list the ingredients and instructions. Since the cooking challenges on *Culinary Chronicles* were always a surprise to the contestants, this seemed like a good way to prepare.

She chose a page at random. "Blancmange."

James snapped his fingers. "Oh, I know that one!" They had made the smooth, white, jelly-like dessert once before. "Let's see. We'll need milk, sugar, vanilla, salt and maybe some cornstarch?"

"And . . ." Alice prompted.

"Gelatin?"

"*Very* important," Hana put in. "The Victorians *loved* gelatin."

Alice cleared her throat, hoping Hana wouldn't make a habit of interrupting their practice. "Okay, now tell me how to make —"

"Except the vegetarians, of course," Hana went on. "You know, gelatin is the reason I turned vegetarian, back when I was fifteen years old. I gave up meat and meat products the moment I found out how gelatin is made!" She laughed. "Do you know how gelatin is made, Alice?"

"Yes," she sighed. And it was the last thing she wanted to talk about. "*Anyway,* back to —"

"Hana, have you told Alice about your research on the suffragettes?" James interrupted.

"They're the women who fought for the right to vote." Hana smiled at her in the rearview mirror.

"I know who they are," Alice returned.

"Apparently, many suffragettes were vegetarian, right, Hana? Isn't that fascinating, Alice?"

"Fascinating," she said through gritted teeth.

"I think so too!" said Hana. "You know, I once wrote an article about a cookbook for suffragettes, which helped women champion the cause in their homes. It's an amazing book — I should have brought it with me."

"Oh, tell us more!" James exclaimed.

Alice let out a strangled sigh, but they didn't seem to hear. She slumped in her seat and stared out the window, watching the city's high-rises disappear behind them and marveling at Hana's ability to ruin a perfectly good moment. She just *had* to bring up the thing Alice hated most about Victorian cooking — the thing that had kept her up at night since Hana had announced they'd be on *Culinary Chronicles.*

Gelatin.

It had all started one October day in the fifth grade. Alice and her classmates had been tasked with researching an interesting profession and presenting their findings to the class. For Alice, the choice was easy: she'd only just moved to her new elementary school and barely knew the other kids, but she doubted any of them knew a culinary historian. She'd even brought in props to show off: a centuries-old cookbook, an antique apple-coring tool and an article her father had written, titled "Politics and the Puff Pastry."

That day, which would feature prominently in her nightmares for months to come, she'd stood in front of her classmates and told them all about her father's life. By day, he taught classes at the university — they'd actually just moved across the city for his new job. And at night, he worked in their kitchen, recreating meals from the past and taking detailed notes in his butter-stained journals. Sometimes he also wrote articles, like the one about the puff pastry, and published them in what he called "academic journals," which as far as Alice could tell were like magazines with no pictures and very few readers.

She ended her presentation by unveiling a big bowl of delicious rice pudding that she and James had made the night before. Rice pudding, she explained, had existed all over the world for a very long time; not even historians knew where it came from originally, though many suspected India. Then she began to dish out generous portions for everyone.

"Ew, it's so slimy!" one kid declared.

"Are those raisins?" Another grimaced. "I don't want any."

Even her teacher, Ms. Kostyniuk, eyed the pudding suspiciously, then declined to eat it on the grounds of her dairy-free diet. "Does anyone have questions about Alice's father's *unusual* job?" she asked the class.

"What's the weirdest thing you ever made?" a boy named Logan demanded. He was presenting after Alice and was already wearing his father's fire chief hat.

She had to think for a moment; they'd made plenty of strange things over the years. "Maybe calf's foot jelly?" In hindsight, she wished she'd chosen any dish but that one.

"EWWWW!" the class chorused.

"That's disgusting!" Logan said gleefully. "How did you make it?"

At that point, she really ought to have stopped talking. But she went on: "It takes a really long time. You have to boil a calf's foot for hours, then take the foot out of the pot and let the liquid turn to jelly. Then you can sweeten it to make it a dessert if you want — it's kind of like how gelatin is made."

"Gelatin?" someone shrieked. "Like in *Jell-o*?"

Alice nodded, and the class erupted into screams.

"That's not true!" cried a girl with pigtails, and she sniffled, as if Alice had just told her that Santa wasn't real. "Jell-o isn't made from cows!"

"Well, no," Alice admitted. "It's usually pigs."

The pigtailed girl began to sob. "It's not true! Ms. Kostyniuk!"

Alice gave Ms. Kostyniuk an exasperated look. Surely she would back her up.

But the teacher's face had turned an odd shade of green. "Thank you, Alice," she said. "I think we've heard enough."

"But . . ." Alice held up the antique apple-coring tool, which she hadn't even demonstrated yet.

"Logan, come tell us about firefighters." Ms. Kostyniuk waved Alice back to her seat.

Logan skipped up to the front of the class, wearing the fire chief hat and a big smirk. "And now for something *way* less weird," he declared, and the class hooted with laughter (except the pigtailed girl, whose head was buried in her arms). Cheeks aflame, Alice slunk back to her desk with a big bowl of rice pudding all to herself.

From that day on, every time Logan and his friends saw her, they would *moo* at the top of their lungs. They called her the calf-boiler, which was neither fair nor accurate, but they wouldn't listen when she tried to explain. She even tried telling Ms. Kostyniuk, but the teacher refused to hear any more about it, and Alice began to wonder if the truth about gelatin had been news to her too.

The torment might have gone on forever had it not been for Cami Diaz, who witnessed the mooing when she arrived to walk Mat home from school one day. She marched over to Logan and his friends, pulled out her cell phone and showed them a video of her flipping a boy at jiu-jitsu practice. If they didn't leave Alice alone, she said, she'd do the same to them.

The moos ceased immediately.

That afternoon, Alice walked home with the Diaz kids, and Cami confirmed her growing suspicion that culinary history wasn't a normal hobby for a ten-year-old. And it *definitely* wasn't cool. "You should keep that stuff on the DL," Cami advised.

"What does that mean?" Alice asked Mat later. She'd been too intimidated to ask Cami herself.

"The down-low," he explained. "It means keep it quiet. She said the same thing about making dioramas," he added sadly.

Eventually, Alice concluded that Cami was right — it was safer to keep her hobby on the down-low. She rarely even talked to Mat about it, though he was her closest friend and might have actually found it interesting. It felt less risky to tell no one. In fact, when Mat had been leaving for art camp, Alice had pretended that she didn't have any plans for the summer at all.

She was about to check her phone again to see if he'd sent a text when she heard Hana mention Mei-Ling Wu.

"So you finally watched it!" said James. "Hana had never seen *Culinary Chronicles* before last night," he told Alice.

"Never?" Alice was surprised.

Hana shook her head. "To be honest, I hadn't even heard of it before I met you. I figured I should get caught up."

"And what did you think?" asked James.

She hesitated. "It was . . . interesting. I really liked Mei-Ling."

"She's Alice's favorite too," said James.

Hana smiled. "I hope we get to meet her. I even started following her on PHOMO."

"You're on PHOMO?" Alice exclaimed just as James groaned, "Not PHOMO again!"

"I love PHOMO!" Hana exclaimed. "It helps me stay in touch with friends who live far away. And there are some really creative accounts — one of my favorites is all about dogs in sweaters."

"Yes!" Alice jabbed the air with her finger. "See, Dad? Hana has an account!"

"Hana's an adult," he pointed out.

She ignored this. "I'll only follow Mat," she promised again. "And the dogs in sweaters. And Mei-Ling Wu."

"There are lots of wonderful food photos on PHOMO, Alice. You might find them inspiring," Hana said. "And of course you can follow my account too."

"Oh. Okay," Alice said. If following Hana meant she could have a PHOMO account, she was willing to do it. "Please, Dad?"

Eventually, James agreed. "This must be how the parents of the nineteenth-century kaleidoscope kids felt," he lamented.

Hana gasped. "Do you know about them?"

He spun toward her. "Do I ever!"

"Let's compare notes!"

They dove into a frenzied conversation that Alice could barely follow. But it didn't matter. She tapped open her phone and began to download PHOMO, feeling once again as though she was about to step into the modern era.

CHAPTER 3

Hana was right: the food photos on PHOMO *were* inspiring. Alice spent the next two hours scrolling through amazing edible creations. She found meringues shaped like jellyfish, macarons that looked exactly like pieces of sushi, and pieces of sushi that looked like panda bears and pineapples. With James's permission, she followed a dozen food accounts and interrupted his conversation regularly to show him mind-boggling creations. She especially loved the videos that showed knives slicing into everyday objects like teapots and alarm clocks, revealing perfect layers of cake inside.

As promised, she followed Mat, Hana, the dogs in sweaters and Mei-Ling Wu. Just the day before, Mei-Ling had posted a picture of herself in a café in Paris, wearing her trademark red high-top sneakers. That had to be an old photo, Alice reasoned, because of course the host was at Gladstone Manor, or would be soon. She scrolled through her photos and imagined what it would be like to meet her. Maybe they'd become such good friends that Mei-Ling would follow her back on PHOMO!

She was still daydreaming about it when Hana turned off the highway and onto a country road surrounded by green fields with red-brick farmhouses.

"Isn't it lovely out here?" said Hana.

Alice took a photo out the window. It turned out blurry — definitely not worthy of posting on PHOMO. "Are we almost there?" she asked as the road twisted around a grove of leafy trees.

"I think so." James gazed out his window. "Gosh, what a beautiful drive."

"Look!" Hana pointed to a wooden sign that said "Gladstone Manor, Next Left" in cream-colored cursive script. "We must be close now."

They turned left onto a gravel road lined with trees, which Hana took at her usual speed, scattering rocks and leaving dust in their wake. Alice gripped her seatbelt, wishing she'd slow down. But then the road twisted one last time, and the trees fell away, revealing —

"Oh my gosh!" Hana stomped on the brakes, launching them all forward in their seats.

"Would you look at that!" James marveled.

Alice gaped. "Is that a *castle*?"

It certainly looked like one. Gladstone Manor was three stories tall and nearly half a city block long, with stone walls the color of perfectly toasted marshmallows, turrets at every corner and at least a dozen chimney stacks reaching into the sky. To the right of the manor was a rose garden bursting with blooms; to the left was a terrace, where people sat under white umbrellas. Manicured lawns stretched for acres on all sides.

As they stared, a man in a suit emerged from the front doors and waved them toward a parking lot, where they parked beside a couple unloading enormous suitcases from their van. Alice grabbed her backpack and cookbooks and climbed out of the car, still gawking at the manor.

"Can you believe this place?" James asked, joining her. "It's a pretty grand setting for *Culinary Chronicles*."

She nodded dumbly. Normally, the show took place in cozy historical houses or dusty little museums — never in castles, or manors that looked like castles.

She hugged the cookbooks to her chest and moved closer to her father.

They hauled their backpacks and Hana's mountain of luggage over to the front doors, which the man in the suit had left open. Inside, they stopped again to stare. The lobby was enormous, paneled floor to ceiling in warm, cocoa-colored wood. To their left, a huge wooden staircase climbed up to the second and third floors. To the right, a chandelier the size of Hana's car dangled hundreds of little crystals over a gleaming grand piano. And next to that stood the biggest fireplace Alice had ever seen, complete with a fire crackling away even though it was mid-July.

And there were people everywhere. Some gathered near the fireplace, sipping wine and laughing. Some were dragging their luggage up the staircase, while others rolled racks of clothing across the room. Then there was a group carrying what looked like lighting equipment; as Alice watched, a man balancing a pole on his shoulder swung around, nearly hitting the chandelier.

"Watch out!" someone cried. "That's two hundred years old!" It was the man in the suit who'd waved at them earlier, and now he was wringing his hands. The man with the pole shrugged and continued on his way.

"Oh dear," fretted the man in the suit, who, Alice noted, was also wearing a bow tie and very pointy shoes. He had a big mustache that curled like a scroll on either side of his mouth.

She wondered if this was a Victorian costume, or just his everyday look.

James whistled. "Close call."

"And not the first one today." The man moaned. Then he straightened and patted his mustache. "Now then. You've just arrived? Come with me!" He led them over to a huge mahogany desk, slipped behind it and turned to face them. "Welcome to Gladstone Manor! You're here for the festival?"

"Kind of," said James. "We're James and Alice Fleck — we're going to be on *Culinary Chronicles*. And this is Hana . . ." He looked around; Hana was off snapping photos of the chandelier. "That's Hana Holmes over there."

"James and Alice . . ." The man donned a pair of gold-rimmed glasses and tapped a few keys on his laptop. "Yes, here you are! I'm Richard Sibley-McFinch." He shook their hands. "I own and run Gladstone Manor."

"This place is incredible," said James.

"Thank you." Richard pulled a handkerchief out of his pocket and wiped his forehead. "It's my pride and joy. Along with Roslyn, of course." He pointed underneath the desk.

"Oh!" Alice hadn't noticed the lean silver dog lying near her sneakers, eyeing them all with suspicion.

"Roslyn is a purebred whippet," said Richard. "You can pet her — she's very friendly."

Alice crouched down and offered the dog a hand to sniff, but Roslyn turned her head away and sighed.

"Gladstone Manor was built in the 1860s," Richard told them. "When I first saw it, it was practically falling apart. But I couldn't resist — Oh! Watch that mirror!" he yelped as a man carrying a tower of boxes nearly walked straight into it. He sighed and wiped his forehead again. "I'm sorry, it's been a

24

stressful day. I thought everything would be in order by the time our guests arrived."

James hummed sympathetically. "It must be an awful lot of work."

Richard nodded. "More than fifty guests are coming for the festival, and that's not including everyone involved in this cooking competition! I had to put the crew up in the stables."

"Wow," said James. "Do you organize a lot of these festivals?"

Richard shook his head. "I love a good costume party, so I've hosted quite a few of those. And I once held a medieval jousting competition — that was murder on the lawn." He grimaced. "But this is my first Victorian festival — I thought it would be easier to manage than a jousting competition. And it might have been, had Gladstone not also been chosen as the venue for this . . . this *production*." He mopped his head with his handkerchief. "I mean, don't get me wrong, it's a huge honor to host *Culinary* —" He stopped suddenly.

"*Chronicles*," Alice offered.

Richard blinked at her, then stuffed his handkerchief back in his pocket. "Yes, of course. Anyway, I should stop talking and get you all checked in. I'm sure you want to get settled." He turned back to his laptop, and James beckoned Hana over.

Alice was relieved when he assigned James and Hana two separate rooms on the second floor — she hadn't even considered how awkward it would be if they all had to room together.

"They're gorgeous rooms. You'll love them," Richard promised. "And for you, Alice, we have a special treat."

"You do?"

"I reserved a corner of the manor just for the kids at the festival! It's just a few rooms," he added, "since there are only three of you. But isn't that fun? It'll be like a big sleepover!"

"Oh." Alice glanced at her father, hoping he'd remember her aversion to sleepovers. She had yet to survive one without having to pretend to be sick and calling him to come pick her up.

"That sounds fun!" Hana cooed.

Alice gave her the stink-eye, then turned back to James. "Do I have to?" she whispered.

"Of course not," he said. "I'm sure there's lots of space in my room, right, Richard?"

"Absolutely, it's one of our largest suites. But wouldn't you rather stay with the other kids? Look, there's one of them now!" Richard pointed across the lobby at a girl who looked to be a year or two older than Alice. She was tall and strong-looking, with red hair that cascaded down her back in perfect waves. It wasn't ginger-colored hair, either — this girl's hair was the color of a red velvet cake. She was taking a selfie with a man and a woman — her parents, Alice assumed — in front of the giant fireplace.

"In fact, she's your roommate, Alice," Richard said. "And get this." He leaned over the desk and whispered, "Her name is *Octavia Sapphire!*"

That settled it. "I'm staying with Dad," said Alice. She had enough to worry about without having to survive a sleepover with Octavia Sapphire, whose hair was like red velvet cake.

Richard handed them their keys and told them that the dining room opened for dinner at six o'clock, in half an hour. Then they hauled their luggage up the staircase to the second floor and turned right, into the east wing of the manor. They followed a long hallway paneled with polished wood and lit by antique lanterns until they reached Hana's room, number 214. James offered to help her settle in, but Alice pulled him on, eager to get to their own room and shut out the world.

"Here we are!" he announced, unlocking the door to room 224. "I bet it'll be . . ."

Alice gasped when the door swung open. "This is *your* room?"

It was larger than the entire ground floor of their townhouse, with light pouring in through elegant arched windows. There were two enormous beds covered with more pillows than James and Alice had ever owned, plus a writing desk in one corner and a green velvet sofa in the middle of the room. The bathroom was the size of Alice's entire bedroom and featured a gleaming copper tub that she could have slept in quite comfortably.

Alice stepped inside, feeling her sneakers sink into the carpet underfoot. "Is this real?"

"I think this is what they call 'the lap of luxury'!" James kicked off his shoes before testing out the sofa. "Glorious. Maybe we should live here forever?"

Alice nodded, though she couldn't even begin to imagine that. She walked over to a window seat overlooking the rose garden and carefully sat down on a cushion. "Dad?"

"Hmm." He was already stretched out on the sofa, eyes closed.

"Is this . . . is this what you expected?"

"Not at all. You?"

She watched a couple strolling through the garden below, hand in hand. "I didn't know what to expect," she said. "But it wasn't this. This is . . . It's . . ." She tried to find the right word.

"Pretty overwhelming?" he finished, sitting up.

She nodded, though she'd been thinking more along the lines of "unsettling" or even a bit "terrifying." As beautiful as Gladstone Manor was, she suddenly wanted to be back at home in their townhouse with its peeling paint and old reading chairs and everything she knew.

"I get that," he said. "But once we start cooking tomorrow, I bet we'll feel more at home."

She swallowed. "I hope so."

"We got this, sous-chef." He sat up and smoothed his wrinkled shirt. "Now, how about we go find some food? Or we could look for Mei-Ling! She has to be around here somewhere."

The thought of Mei-Ling Wu made Alice smile. But the thought of returning to the lobby made her shudder. She'd only just found a place where she could hear herself think. "Maybe I'll stay here."

"You don't want to explore? You're not hungry?"

She shook her head.

"All right, I'll see if Hana wants to come. You don't mind staying by yourself for a bit?"

"Oh." She hadn't actually expected him to go without her. "Um, no. I'll be fine."

"I'll bring you some food in case you get hungry later," he promised, slipping his shoes back on.

Then he left, and Alice found herself alone. And suddenly, the room was a little *too* quiet.

At least you're not having a week-long sleepover, she reminded herself. She wouldn't have to worry about what Octavia Sapphire would think about her taking part in *Culinary Chronicles.* And the other kid too — Richard had said there were three of them, including Alice.

The sun ducked behind a cloud, darkening the room. She shivered and hopped up from the window seat to flick on some lights. Then she grabbed her phone, and a cookbook from her backpack, and headed for one of the beds. It turned out to be even softer than it looked. She settled in under the covers and tapped open her PHOMO app.

She wasn't sure how long she spent watching videos of knives slicing into alarm clocks that turned out to be cake, but eventually she fell fast asleep with her phone beside her on the pillow.

CHAPTER
4

"Alice, have you seen my scarf?"

Alice paused with her toothbrush in her mouth. "What scarf?"

"You know, the lucky one!"

She joined her father beside his bed, where he was digging through his suitcase, tossing clothes every which way. She unzipped the front pocket and pulled out the scarf. "It was the last thing you packed, remember?"

"Ah." He smiled. "What would I do without you, sous-chef?"

"You'd probably have terrible luck." She handed him his scarf.

"The absolute worst," he agreed.

She watched him knot the scarf around his neck. He'd had it for as long as she could remember, and its age was definitely starting to show: the fabric, once emerald-green, was sun-bleached and frayed. But he still wore it on important occasions, insisting it brought him good luck.

"I found this on a train, you know," he said.

"In the Pyrenees mountains," she continued. "Where you were a university student studying cave-aged cheese."

"Have I told you this story before?"

"Maybe a few times. Or a few hundred."

He laughed, and Alice resumed brushing her teeth. Truth be told, she'd always had her doubts about the lucky scarf. She hadn't been around back when her father had been studying cave-aged cheese in the Pyrenees, but she knew a bit about the time he'd spent there, and it didn't sound all that lucky. Still, the scarf made him happy, and if ever there was a day for good luck charms, this was it. Alice wouldn't have minded one herself. She'd woken early that morning (still wearing the previous day's clothes) with her stomach in knots. At eight o'clock sharp, they'd be meeting the other competitors. At nine o'clock, they'd start cooking.

As Alice had lain in bed, waiting for James's alarm to go off, she'd made a list of everything that could go wrong that day. They might have to make a recipe they'd never heard of. Or she might embarrass herself in front of Mei-Ling Wu. Worse yet, she might drop some crucial ingredient on the floor and mess up the entire recipe.

"It's going to be fine, Alice," James said, and she realized that she was standing in the middle of the room, clutching her toothbrush. "It's going to be *fun*. That's why we're here."

"Fun. Yes." She returned to the bathroom to braid her hair for a third time.

By seven-thirty, they were back in the lobby of Gladstone Manor, which was thankfully empty and quiet, since most of the guests had yet to emerge from their rooms. James led Alice past the grand piano and the fireplace and down the hall to the dining room, which he'd found while exploring the previous day. A breakfast buffet awaited them, complete with ham, bacon, eggs, crumpets, porridge, pastries and even fried fish.

James devoured a plate of ham and eggs while Alice picked at a croissant and gazed around at the sky-blue wallpaper, the crisp white tablecloths and the other diners in the room. A few tables over, two men chatted excitedly as they buttered a pile of crumpets. Near the window, a girl sat by herself, nibbling a slice of melon. She looked to be sixteen or seventeen years old, and Alice wondered if she might be the third kid in the kids-only wing.

"You have to see the library on the third floor," James told her as he mowed through his ham and eggs. "The bookshelves reach from floor to ceiling — they're probably ten feet tall. I could spend hours in there!"

Alice noted that the men with the crumpets were wearing matching aquamarine neckties. Were they dressed up for the festival, she wondered, or were they competing on *Culinary Chronicles*?

"I didn't get a chance to peek into the Great Hall, where the competition takes place," James went on. "But I saw tons of production people milling around it. You know, I would never have guessed that so much effort goes into making this show. It looks like such a small production on TV."

"James and Alice?"

They looked up to see a young woman dressed all in black and holding a clipboard.

"I'm Jasmina," she said. "I'm a producer on *Culinary Chronicles*."

"So nice to meet you!" James hopped to his feet and shook her hand. "We're huge fans of the show."

"All the contestants are meeting in the parlor, where we'll get to know each other and talk about how the competition works. Are you ready to go?" Jasmina asked.

"Absolutely," said James.

Alice abandoned her croissant and followed them to the door. On the way, they picked up the girl, who was introduced to them as Diana, and the two men, Samir and Sven. Along with their matching neckties, the men were wearing identical white button-up shirts. Alice looked down at her shorts and T-shirt, then over at her father's scarf, which was now flecked with bits of egg. She wondered if they ought to have spent more time thinking about their outfits.

Jasmina led them back to the lobby, then over to the east wing and into the parlor. It was bright and airy, with mint-green walls, rose-colored sofas and a chandelier that scattered rainbows of light all over the room.

Alice and James sat down next to a pair of middle-aged women with identical black curls, identical smiles and matching cupcake-print sweatshirts — one blue and one yellow. Beside them sat an older woman in a tweed blazer and a balding man in a flamingo-print shirt. Alice looked around for Mei-Ling Wu, but the host was nowhere to be seen.

"Looks like we're all here!" Jasmina said, checking her clipboard. "Welcome, everyone. This is a big day for us all. We have a lot to go over, but let's start with introductions. Oh, and we'll be filming this — that's Meg, our lead videographer." She pointed to a woman with a hefty video camera, who grinned and waved.

Alice shivered at the sight of the camera and inched closer to her father.

The introductions began. Sven and Samir explained that they owned a popular catering company in the city — Sven was the head chef, and Samir kept the business running smoothly. They'd always wanted to try cooking competitively and thought that *Culinary Chronicles* would be an easy place to start.

The women in the cupcake-print sweatshirts were identical twins named Antonia and Valentina, but they preferred Toni and Tina. Tina professed to being a big fan of the show, and Toni admitted to never having watched it before.

Phyllis in the tweed blazer was a culinary historian like James, and she would be competing without an assistant. So would François, in the flamingo-print shirt. He confessed that he knew next to nothing about Victorian food but was obsessed with cooking shows.

Diana, the girl from the dining hall, would also be competing alone. She explained, so quietly that everyone had to lean in to hear, that she'd just finished high school and would turn eighteen in a month. Alice guessed this meant she was not staying in the kids' wing. And it made Alice the youngest competitor by far.

When it was James and Alice's turn, James told everyone that they had been cooking together as chef and sous-chef since Alice was old enough to hold a spoon. Normally Alice didn't mind it when he said that, but today it made her face flush. She took a few deep breaths and tried not to look at the video camera.

Once the introductions were over, Jasmina went on to explain that she would also be acting as their handler, meaning she'd make sure they had everything they needed and were in the right place at the right time. "I'm here to help, as much as I can," she told them. "So now, let's move on to the rules."

Alice tried hard to focus. Rules were very important.

"Rule Number One is that from now on, you have to keep everything that happens secret until the show airs in the fall. People can know that you're on the show, but they can't know what happens during the challenges or who wins. Okay? I'll get you to sign a nondisclosure agreement a bit later."

"What's that?" Alice whispered to James.

"Just a form that says we promise not to tell," he whispered back.

"I guess this means we can't post to PHOMO?" François sounded disappointed.

"Definitely not," Jasmina confirmed.

"What about the guests in the manor?" asked Sven. "Won't they find out?"

Jasmina sighed. "We have to get them to sign the agreement too. It's overly complicated if you ask me, but the executives liked the idea of this festival thing as a backdrop." She waved her hand around the room, looking rather put out.

"Rule Number Two," Jasmina went on. "No cell phones allowed — you'll have to leave them with me. I'll give them back after each challenge." She held out her hands, and the competitors reluctantly passed over their phones.

"Now, let's go over the schedule." She explained that the show would be filmed over the next seven days, and they'd compete every day except Day Two and Day Five. "On those days, you can rest or enjoy this festival thing, if you're into that. Sound good?"

The competitors agreed that rest days were much appreciated.

"Great. And now . . ." She paused, then gave them a smile that looked both tired and forced. "We have a surprise for you." She glanced at Meg, the videographer. "Ready?"

Alice felt her stomach tighten. She was not a big fan of surprises.

"As I'm sure you know," Jasmina went on, "*Culinary Chronicles* has always aired on the History Alive network, which . . . well, let's just say it doesn't get the most viewers."

"I love the History Alive network," Phyllis piped up.

"I do too," James added.

"Right. Well, some executives at RealiTV recently decided to purchase the rights to the show. This came as a huge surprise to all of us who work on it, since RealiTV is a very popular streaming service. You guys are probably familiar with its shows, like *Why Are You Wearing That?* and *Dog Show Divas.*"

François gasped. "I love *Dog Show Divas!*"

"RealiTV?" Alice whispered. She turned to James. "*RealiTV?*"

"I don't know what that is," he said quietly. "Do you?"

Alice nodded. The Diaz family subscribed to RealiTV so Cami could watch her favorite show, in which hockey players were forced to take up competitive ice dancing. RealiTV, according to Cami, was cool. A *lot* of people watched it.

Including people Alice's age.

Her heart began to pound.

"Wait, so, what does this mean?" asked Samir. "Has the show changed?"

"In some ways," Jasmina said carefully. "You see, the RealiTV executives decided it was time to shake things up, to give *Culinary Chronicles* a new look and feel. And they started by . . ." — she paused, then swallowed — "finding a new host."

Everyone gasped.

"You got rid of Mei-Ling Wu?" cried Sven.

The producer looked pained. "We *loved* Mei-Ling. But the executives thought the show needed more of a . . . a reality TV personality. So they hired Miranda Summers. You might know her as the host of *Why Are You Wearing That?*"

"Oh no," Samir moaned.

Alice had no idea who Miranda Summers was, but she knew this was not good news. In fact, it was terrible. She turned to her father. "No Mei-Ling?"

He squeezed her hand. "It's going to be okay," he assured her.

But there was more.

"Then the executives insisted we hire a new judge. And this is really exciting," Jasmina added, looking about as excited as someone awaiting major dental surgery.

"Exciting?" Alice mouthed to James. They had agreed to be on *Culinary Chronicles* precisely because it *wasn't* exciting!

"They hired the one and only..." — Jasmina glanced at Meg again — "Tom Truffleman."

"WHAT!" yelled François.

"Tom *Truffleman?*" cried Samir.

"Even *I* know who that is!" Toni exclaimed. She turned to her sister. "*Tom Truffleman* is going to be judging us? What are we doing here?"

Alice gripped her father's hand. "Who's that?"

"Tom Truffleman," Samir informed her, "is the fiercest judge in the world of competitive cooking. He's judged shows like *Bare-knuckled Bakers* and *Feast or Failure*. He's notoriously impossible to please."

"He almost never has anything good to say," added Sven.

"We're going to be on a Tom Truffleman show?" François threw his arms in the air. "This is amazing! We'll all be famous!"

"Now wait just a minute here," Phyllis snapped. "We came to participate in *Culinary Chronicles* and cook authentic Victorian dishes. And now you're telling us everything has changed?"

"Not everything," Jasmina said quickly. "You'll still be cooking Victorian dishes, at least as far as I know. It's just that Tom Truffleman might have ... different expectations. He has very high standards for the competitors on his shows."

Alice thought she heard Diana whimper.

"I'm sure you can all do this," the producer said. "Maybe . . . it'll even be fun?"

Alice was quite sure it would not. She was also quite sure she was going to be sick.

"Oh, I almost forgot about the prize!" Jasmina snapped her fingers. "The winner will have the opportunity to write and publish their own cookbook! Pretty cool, right?" She gave them a hopeful look.

"*Very* cool," said François.

Alice said nothing. She'd never considered writing a cookbook before and didn't care to think about it now.

"And I have just one more surprise for you," said Jasmina.

"What *now*?!" everyone cried.

She clutched her clipboard. "The show isn't called *Culinary Chronicles* anymore. You'll be participating in *Culinary Combat.*"

A stunned silence ensued, followed a moment later by a thud that shook the parlor. Everyone spun around to see Diana sprawled on the floor.

CHAPTER 5

"**S**he's fainted!" Tina cried.

"I'll get some water!" Samir dashed for the door.

"Turn off that camera!" Phyllis snapped at Meg.

Alice leapt to her feet, but Diana was already surrounded by people trying to revive her — and capture the scene on video. She hung back, leaning against her father and trying to think through everything she'd just learned. Mei-Ling Wu had lost her job. *Culinary Chronicles* was now *Culinary Combat*. And it would be broadcast on RealiTV for the entire world to see.

Part of her wished she too were unconscious.

Diana made a mewling noise, like an abandoned kitten.

"She's coming to!" Sven yelled as Samir ran back in with a glass of water.

"Thank god," Jasmina said to her clipboard. "We have to start filming in less than half an hour."

"This is bonkers," Alice breathed. She felt like she was watching a TV show — which, she realized, was exactly what was happening. All of this would be on TV.

"Dad." She turned to face him. "I can't do this."

"It's a bit crazy, isn't it?" he said, watching as the twins helped Diana sit up.

It was worse than that. "We need to get out of here. Like, right now." Her throat felt dangerously tight; if they didn't escape soon, she was most definitely going to cry.

"Hey." James crouched to look her in the eye. "It's okay, sous-chef. We can do this, I'm sure of it."

But there was a wrinkle forming between his eyebrows. Alice knew that wrinkle — it meant he wasn't sure at all.

She took a shaky breath. "I agreed to be on *Culinary Chronicles*, a show that no one watches. I didn't sign up for *Culinary . . .*" she could barely say it, "*Combat.*"

"Yes, but —"

"We shouldn't be here," she insisted. And it suddenly occurred to her that they *wouldn't* be there if it weren't for Hana. *Hana* had gotten them into this mess by sending in their application without even asking them. Alice's hands clenched into fists. Of course, this was all Hana's fault.

"Look." James squeezed her shoulders. "I know this isn't what we thought we were getting ourselves into. But remember, Jasmina said we'll still be cooking Victorian dishes, and we're very good at that. Also, these people seem nice, don't you think?" He gestured at the other contestants.

"I'm not worried about them!" said Alice. "I'm worried about *Tom Truffleman.* The fiercest judge in the world of competitive cooking, remember?"

"Right, him." James frowned. "Well, maybe he won't be that bad. And anyway," he hurried on before Alice could argue that he might actually be *worse*, "we're in this together. We're a great team. I really think it's going to be okay."

Now Diana was back on her feet, insisting she was fine, and Jasmina was sighing with relief. "Let's head to the Great Hall, everyone!" The producer led them toward the door. "I'll explain more once we get there."

Exchanging uneasy glances, the competitors fell in line behind her.

They reached the lobby just as Richard Sibley-McFinch stepped through the front door, with Roslyn the silver whippet in his arms. "Good morning, competitors!" he cried. "What an exciting day it — Oh!" He stopped when he saw the twins propping up poor Diana. "Is everything okay?"

"She'll be fine," Jasmina assured him. "The news was just surprising."

"Oh dear." Richard stroked the whippet's head, as if she were the one who needed soothing.

He'd known about the surprise all along, Alice realized. When he'd checked them in the previous day, he'd been keeping it secret. How many others had been in on it, she wondered, and how long had they known?

Jasmina led them back to the west wing and into the Great Hall, which turned out to be just what it sounded like: a great big hall. It had shiny wood floors and wine-colored walls decorated with enormous oil paintings framed in gold.

But what caught Alice's attention were the workstations. There were six of them grouped in the middle of the room, each equipped with an oven, stovetop, sink and cupboards. Off to one side stood three refrigerators and a huge set of shelves lined with cooking supplies.

And there were people *everywhere*: setting up lights, testing microphones, wiping down countertops, arranging ingredients on the shelves. There were no fewer than six videographers, plus an entire team of makeup artists wielding brushes and powder puffs. Without a word, they descended on the competitors and set to work.

"Oh!" James flinched as a very tall man began to powder his nose. "Do I really need that?"

"Absolutely." The man swept a brush across his forehead. "Are you actually going to wear that scarf?"

"My scarf? Oh yes, I have to. It's good luck."

The man frowned. "Give it here."

When James hesitated, he held out his hand. Sighing, James took off the scarf and passed it over. With a flick of his wrists, the man twisted it expertly, like a cowboy wielding a lasso, then knotted it around James's neck. "That's better."

"It is?" James looked at Alice.

"Actually, yes," she said. She wasn't sure what the man had done, but the old scarf now looked far more stylish.

The makeup artist then turned to her and whipped a bottle of hairspray out of his apron. "Flyaways," he tsked, spritzing her head. "But that's all you need. You have the skin of a twelve-year-old."

"I *am* a twelve-year-old," she told him, but he'd already moved on to spritz and powder someone else.

Once all the competitors had been deemed "camera ready," Jasmina assigned them each a workstation. They were arranged in two rows of three; Alice and James got the middle spot on the right, with Sven and Samir in front of them and François behind.

"Would you look at these tools!" James whistled, rifling through the cupboards. "All brand-new, and such high quality!"

Alice nodded. The workstation had every kind of pot, bowl, cake pan or pie plate they could ever need, and everything sparkled in a way that their own kitchen tools never had and certainly never would. Even the oven mitts were made of high-quality silicone, unlike the old fabric mitts they had at home, which were riddled with holes from all the times they'd accidentally burned them.

"And *look!*" James pointed at a cherry-red Superchef stand-mixer sitting on the counter.

Alice caught her breath. It was the stand-mixer of her dreams, and one they could never afford — she knew this because she'd been asking for one for years. She'd even written to Santa about it when she was six years old, but to her disappointment, he'd brought her an old eggbeater instead ("It's an eighteenth century antique!" James had explained).

She reached out to touch the Superchef, imagining the egg whites she could whip so effortlessly. Then she pulled her hand away, because it wasn't right. It wasn't fair! Here was her chance to finally use a Superchef, and all she wanted to do was run away.

"Okay, everyone!" Jasmina clapped her hands for attention. "Here's how this is going to work. Just like on *Culinary Chronicles*, your task is to create a dish in a limited amount of time. You'll have a recipe, but it might be short on details, so you'll have to fill in the blanks yourself. Tom Truffleman and Miranda Summers will be walking around as you work, and if they stop at your station, you should try to have a conversation with them. I know that can be challenging when you're trying to stay focused, but do your best. Oh, and Tom will undoubtedly try to intimidate you. But don't let it bother you — it's just his way."

"Maybe he won't be that bad, right?" Alice muttered to James, but he was busy pulling aprons out of a drawer.

"Do you think the blue or the gray goes best with my scarf?" he asked, holding them both up.

She refused to answer.

Next came the microphones, which were clipped to their collars and tucked out of sight.

"Remember, your mic will be on at all times in the Great Hall," one member of the production crew warned them. "Whatever you say will be recorded and possibly used on the show. So no swearing," he added with a grin.

James chuckled. Alice saw nothing funny about it. She'd never even considered having to wear a microphone that would record everything she said. Could it possibly get any worse?

"And now it's time to meet our host and judge!" Jasmina waved to a man waiting near the doors, and he promptly pushed them open. "Everyone, meet Miranda Summers and Tom Truffleman!"

They strode into the Great Hall arm in arm. Tom Truffleman had white hair cropped close to his head and dark-rimmed glasses on his nose, and he wore a powder-blue suit that shimmered when he moved. Miranda Summers wore a red, ruffled dress and high heels so sharp and thin they might have doubled as cake-testers. Her long, blond ponytail swished as she walked through the hall, smiling at every video camera and completely ignoring the contestants.

Alice thought about Mei-Ling Wu, who would have arrived in her red high-top sneakers and surely would have given each one of them a hug. Where was Mei-Ling now? she wondered. Had she found a new job yet?

"Welcome, Tom and Miranda," Jasmina said. "I'd like to introduce you to —"

"What's going on here?" Tom dropped Miranda's arm, and she wobbled on her heels. "Why are some of them paired up?"

Jasmina took a deep breath. "We went over this, Tom. Remember? Each participant was allowed to bring an assistant if they wanted. That's how it worked on *Culinary Chronicles*."

He huffed. "Well, that's not how it works on my shows. All competitors should fend for themselves!"

Alice let out a squeak.

"Wait . . ." Tom Truffleman whipped off his glasses. "Is that a *kid*? She's not competing, is she?"

Alice's knees buckled, and she grabbed the countertop. James laid a hand on her shoulder.

"Kids do not belong on my show!" The judge looked indignant.

"We talked about this too, Tom," Jasmina reminded him. "Kids were allowed to take part in *Culinary Chronicles*. It just didn't happen very often because, well, not many kids watched the show."

Alice felt her cheeks turn tomato-red.

"Anyway, Alice is a very experienced cook." Jasmina gave her an encouraging look.

"Very experienced!" James added. "Alice and I have been cooking together since she was old enough to hold a spoon."

Tom Truffleman pursed his lips. "Look, no offense to the kid, but when I was just starting out in this business, *many* years ago, I had to judge a kids' cooking show." He grimaced. "It was called *Kids Can Cook (Or Can They Really?)*. And — spoiler alert — they can't."

"Tom," Jasmina said through gritted teeth. "We need to talk. Off set."

He huffed again but followed Jasmina to a corner for a private conversation.

"How rude," Tina whispered from across the aisle. "Don't be intimidated by him, Alice. You'll show him."

"We will indeed." Her father patted her shoulder.

"I wish we hadn't come," she moaned, watching Tom Truffleman waving his arms at Jasmina. Miranda Summers, meanwhile, had yet to even glance in their direction.

"All right." Jasmina marched back on set. "We've agreed to keep things as they are for now. *Everyone* will stay."

"But know this!" Tom Truffleman declared. "You are competing on a Tom Truffleman show, and I have high expectations. Let me tell you what I want." He held up a hand and counted his demands on his fingers. "Technical perfection! Balanced flavors! Magnificent taste! Creative flair! In short, I want perfection."

"Wow, no pressure or anything," Samir murmured.

Phyllis piped up. "And what about historical accuracy?"

Tom Truffleman blinked at her. "You can be as historically accurate as you want as long as your creation doesn't bore me. I absolutely hate being bored."

Alice looked around at the other competitors, whose expressions ranged from concerned to terrified. Diana looked as though she might faint again at any minute.

"Well, on that note, let's get started!" Jasmina clapped her hands. "We'll roll in three minutes! Places, everyone!"

Alice turned to her father and quietly informed him that she was going to throw up.

"You won't," he said.

"I think I will." It was a problem she hadn't considered when she'd listed all the potential calamities that morning. Supposing she threw up all over their workstation?

"Sous-chef." He put an arm around her shoulders. "We can do this. If there's one thing we know how to do, it's cook together."

"One minute till we roll!" someone called.

"We can do this," James assured her again, and though Alice was not convinced, she also knew it was too late to escape. She was going to compete whether she liked it or not. All she could do was tighten her apron strings and brace herself for whatever was about to happen.

CHAPTER
6

"Welcome to *Culinary Combat*. I'm your host, Miranda Summers." She gave the video camera a wide smile. "You might know me from reality TV shows like the smash hit *Why Are You Wearing That?* and its spin-off series, *What Were You Thinking When You Got That Haircut?*"

Alice thought again about Mei-Ling Wu, who at the very least would have wished the competitors good luck before the filming began. Miranda Summers probably didn't even know their names.

"We're here today at the beautiful Gladstone Manor," Miranda went on, "to kick off the very first season of *Culinary Combat*, a brand-new show featuring none other than Tom Truffleman!" She waved at the judge. He gave the camera a stern look, as if it had already failed to meet his high expectations.

Miranda laughed. "Typical Truffleman! You competitors better watch out!"

Alice stole a glance at Diana, who still looked pale despite the pink powder the makeup crew had piled on her cheeks. But at least she was standing upright.

"Now, these people just got the surprise of their lives," Miranda told the cameras. "They thought they were taking part in a friendly little competition that almost no one would watch!" She threw her head back and laughed again. "They might still be recovering from the shock. But there's no time for that, because the battle is about to begin!" She gave the camera her biggest smile yet. Alice's mouth ached just watching it.

She turned to her father and mouthed, "I'm going to be sick."

"You won't," he mouthed back, although he too was looking a bit green.

"And we're not done with surprises yet!" the host proclaimed. "I'm about to tell the competitors what they'll be making today and how much time they'll have. When that time is up, Tom Truffleman will judge their creations and decide who made it best . . . and who will leave the hall in shame. Ready to find out, guys?"

Alice held her breath, praying it wouldn't be something weird, like jellied eels or pig's head or —

"You'll have exactly an hour and fifteen minutes to bake . . . a Victoria punch cake!"

"A *what?*" Alice looked at James, then at the other contestants. All looked equally blank.

"Cut!" called Jasmina. "It's a *sponge* cake, Miranda. A Victoria *sponge* cake. Try it again." She turned to the contestants. "Sorry, guys. Try to look surprised, okay?"

Miranda cleared her throat and turned back to the camera. "You have an hour and fifteen minutes to bake . . . a Victoria *sponge* cake!"

For a moment, no one moved. And then everyone moved at once. The competitors fumbled for their recipes, opened their cupboards, fiddled with the dials on their ovens. Cameras fanned out across the room.

And Alice found, to her horror, that she had no idea what to do. And what's more, she couldn't move, not even a muscle. As the camera crew scurried around the room and the other competitors began making their cakes, she could only watch, completely overwhelmed and absolutely certain she was going to cry. And then she would be forever remembered as the kid who cried on TV — and maybe threw up too.

"Well, this is lucky," James said cheerfully, opening the top drawer of their workstation. "You quizzed me on this recipe last week, remember?"

Alice tried to remember but couldn't. And now there was a video camera beside her, zooming in on her blank expression. She gripped the countertop again.

James pulled the recipe out of the drawer and set it on the counter. "Hmm."

"What is it?" She braced herself for the worst.

"There are details missing. We'll have to guess the oven temperature and how long to bake the cake. But all the ingredients are here, at least as far as I can remember. How about you?"

She glanced at the recipe, but the words swam on the page. "I . . . I can't."

"No problem. Just follow along," he murmured as he set the oven to 400 degrees. "It'll get easier as we settle in. Now, let's go find our ingredients."

Alice took a deep breath and tried to follow along as they collected their ingredients from the shelves, then returned to the workstation to make their sponge cake. But it didn't get easier. All the motions that felt so natural at home — measuring flour, greasing cake pans, creaming butter — now felt strange and clumsy, as if she were attempting them for the very first time. Blindfolded. In quicksand.

And to make things even worse, the cameras were *everywhere*. They followed her to the shelves and filmed her gathering flour and sugar. They caught her tripping over her feet on her way back to the workstation. They hovered nearby as she stared at the Superchef mixer, trying to figure out how to turn it on. And they captured her blushing when she realized she hadn't plugged it in.

Meanwhile, mixers whirred all around them, the production crew zipped about, and competitors dashed to the shelves and back to their stations. With all that noise and commotion, Alice could barely concentrate long enough to spoon flour into a measuring cup.

Thankfully, James seemed undeterred. "Now for the eggs," he said once they'd creamed their butter and sugar together in the Superchef. He handed one to Alice, but she hesitated, suddenly unsure she could even crack an egg. But he insisted, so she took it. And she was just about to tap it on the rim of the bowl when she noticed Tom Truffleman approaching — slowly, like a powder-blue predator.

Alice's whole body tightened, including her grip on the egg. "Oh!" she yelped as it shattered in her hand. She dropped the whole thing into their bowl.

"Oh no!" James exclaimed, then quickly cleared his throat. "I mean, it's fine. No problems here," he told Tom Truffleman.

The judge peered into the bowl. "Except for those eggshells."

Alice's hand flew to her mouth. She'd just shattered an egg in front of the fiercest judge in the world of competitive cooking! Two cameras descended on their station to film the mess.

"Don't worry," James said, though it wasn't clear whether he was talking to Alice or Tom Truffleman. "We'll pick the eggshells out. And if we can't, we'll just start again. No problem." He squeezed Alice's shoulder.

"You think you have time to start over?" The judge glanced at the clock on the wall. Fifteen minutes had already passed.

"We're on it!" James removed the mixing bowl from the Superchef, then grabbed a spoon and got to work. Within a minute, he'd plucked all the bits of eggshell out of the batter. Tom Truffleman sauntered off to intimidate someone else.

"You're sure you got them all?" Alice fretted as James added a teaspoon of vanilla to their batter. "Like, totally sure?"

"As sure as I can be."

"But are you —"

"Alice, it's fine. We just have to keep going."

"It's just that I . . ." She bit her lip, wanting to say, "I might have ruined everything." But she knew that if she said it, she'd start crying for sure.

"You didn't," James said. "Now, did I ever tell you about Queen Victoria's dinner parties?"

"About what?" She sniffed.

"The Queen's dinner parties," he said, adding the dry ingredients to the wet ones. "Of course, you already know that this cake was named for Queen Victoria. But did you know she had an absolutely voracious appetite?"

"Um, no," said Alice, who couldn't imagine why he'd chosen this moment to tell her about the Queen's appetite.

He handed her a spoon and motioned for her to stir. "Back then, the Queen was always served first at a banquet. Everyone else was served in order of social status, from the most important person to the least. At a big party, the least important person could be kept waiting a *very* long time."

Alice listened as she stirred the batter, being careful not to overmix it, since overmixing could spell disaster for a sponge cake.

"Victoria would throw massive banquets for hundreds of guests, and she wasted no time tucking into her food, devouring it with gusto. By the time she was finished eating, say, her soup, some guests would have only just received theirs. But a guest wasn't allowed to eat if the Queen wasn't eating, so their soup would be whisked away before they could even taste it. Dinners with the Queen were not exactly relaxing."

Alice heard the twins chuckle across the aisle, and she looked up from her batter to discover that most of the competitors — even some of the production crew — were listening to James.

And not only that, but for the first time that day, Alice herself was breathing normally. She didn't even feel like throwing up.

"Thanks, Dad," she whispered as they poured their batter into two cake pans.

"Any time." He slid the pans into the oven. "More on Victoria later. Right now, we have to decide how long this needs to bake."

The answer came immediately. "Twenty minutes."

He grinned. "Just enough time to make the jam."

"I'll get the berries." She dashed to the fridges, grabbed two pints of raspberries, then sprinted back to their station just as Miranda Summers sashayed over with a videographer in tow.

"It's the father-daughter duo!" she cooed. "That's so cute. It's James, right? And Allie?"

"Alice," they corrected her.

Miranda gave her a once-over. "Allie, how old are you?"

"Twelve," she replied, hoping that would be the last question she'd have to answer.

"Twelve!" Miranda leaned against the countertop, and Alice grabbed the raspberries before she could squash them. "That's wild. What do your friends think of this? I mean, Victorian cooking isn't exactly a normal hobby for a twelve-year-old, is it?" She giggled. "It wasn't in my time, anyway. And believe me, that wasn't very long ago."

"Oh. Um, they don't actually know about it," she mumbled.

James jumped in. "This was a big surprise for everyone. We had no idea we were going to be on *Culinary Combat*, so naturally Alice's friends don't know either."

It wasn't what Alice had meant, but she appreciated the help. She handed him the raspberries and prayed Miranda would leave.

But the host didn't move. "And what about Allie's mother? Is she here too?"

Oh no, Alice groaned inwardly.

"Nope." James shook his head as he mashed up the raspberries. "It's just me and Alice."

"You're single?!" Miranda's hands flew to her cheeks, as if he'd just announced his intention to fly to the moon by flapping his arms. "James, are you telling me you're an *eligible bachelor*?"

Around the room, heads swiveled their way. Alice wished she could crawl into one of the cupboards.

"This is so exciting," the host bubbled. "As I'm sure you know, I got my big break as a contestant on the hit reality show *Eligible*." She winked at the camera.

"Did you?" James said as he strained the raspberries through a sieve. Alice knew he was trying to sound polite but had

54

actually never heard of the show. She'd never watched it herself, but she knew it involved a single person choosing from a number of suitors over the course of a season. Which sounded completely ridiculous.

"Well, I'm not really an eligible bachelor," James told Miranda. "I'm in a relationship."

If she could fit in one of the cupboards, Alice decided, she would never emerge.

Miranda's face fell. But before she could say anything more, Jasmina began waving her arms and pointing to the clock.

"What? Oh! Twelve more minutes!" Miranda cried. The contestants all gasped.

"Let's see if our cakes are ready." James slipped on the fancy silicone oven mitts. But just as he was about to open the oven, François let out a shriek.

"What's the matter?" called Tina.

"M-my oven!" he stammered. "It's . . . it's off!"

"No!" Alice spun around to see François standing in front of his oven, his hands in oven mitts pressed to his cheeks.

"You forgot to set it?" Phyllis asked as she took two perfectly golden cakes out of her oven.

"No, I did!" François wailed. "At least, I thought I did!"

If this had been *Culinary Chronicles*, Mei-Ling would have swooped in to console him. Miranda did no such thing; in fact, she'd wandered off set to have her face powdered again.

"Can we help him?" Alice asked James. "He could use our oven, since it's already hot."

James glanced at the clock and sighed. "It's too late — there's only ten minutes left." Just as the words left his mouth, their oven timer beeped. They pulled their cakes out and pressed their fingers gently onto the golden tops. "Perfect," James whispered when the cakes sprang right back up.

They let the cakes sit for a few minutes, then turned them out of the pans to cool for a few minutes more. Then they spread jam on top of one cake and carefully placed the other on top of that, like a giant jam sandwich.

"I'd say it's the ideal Victoria sponge cake," James proclaimed.

Alice stepped back to study their creation. He was right: it was the ideal Victoria sponge cake. Or, it would have been for *Culinary Chronicles*.

But this was *Culinary Combat*. And Tom Truffleman had very different expectations.

If she had more time, she could have built an impressive cake-topper, like a capital V made of choux pastry or meringue. But only four minutes remained. All she could do was make the cake look interesting. She yanked open a drawer and grabbed a roll of parchment paper. "Do we have scissors?"

James found a pair and handed them over. "What now? We've only got —"

"I know." She snipped the paper into the shape of a crown and placed it in the middle of the cake. Then she ran to the shelf, grabbed a bag of powdered sugar and ran back to their station, where she sifted the sugar onto the cake. Once the cloud of sugar had fallen, she carefully peeled back the parchment paper, leaving an imprint of a crown.

"Sous-chef!" James exclaimed. "That's beautiful!"

"Thanks." She liked it too. But would Tom Truffleman?

"Time's up, everyone!" Miranda called, stepping back on set with a freshly powdered face.

"Well, we did it," said James. "And we averted all disasters."

Alice nodded, suddenly exhausted. She leaned on the counter while the cleaning crew scrubbed the workstations until they sparkled as they had before the challenge began. Others set up a table at the front of the room, where Tom Truffleman would judge the sponge cakes.

He called Diana up first. She went shakily, gripping her cake plate with white knuckles.

Truffleman took a tiny bite and chewed it thoughtfully. "It's dry," he said eventually. "You must have left it in the oven too long. And it's dull too. Definitely not a memorable cake."

"Oh." Diana bit her lip.

"Yes." Truffleman patted his mouth with a napkin. "I'll never think about that cake again. Next!"

Diana opened her mouth, then closed it. She picked up her cake and returned to her station, looking dazed.

The twins went next, carrying what looked like a perfect Victoria sponge: the cake was fluffy and golden, the jam in between looked thick and smooth.

"A decent cake," Truffleman said after a bite and a pause. "Decent jam." Then he sighed. "But, just like that last one, it's unremarkable. I've basically already forgotten it." He shook his head. "Who's next?"

Toni's mouth fell open. "That's it? After all that work?"

Tina shushed her. She thanked the judge, then steered her sister back to their station.

Alice looked at James with wide eyes. If the twins' beautiful cake was unremarkable, what were they in for? He could only shrug.

Next came François, with two cake pans filled with uncooked batter. "I'm sorry —" he began.

"Those are *raw!*" Tom Truffleman recoiled at the sight. "Are you actually trying to serve me *raw cake?*"

"Ew!" Miranda stepped away, as if the cakes might rise up to attack her.

"Of course not! I just had a bit of bad luck." François's face was as pink as the flamingos on his shirt. "I could have sworn I'd turned on my oven . . ."

"You forgot to turn on your oven." Tom Truffleman shook his head in disgust. "What is this, a cooking show for kids? You've disappointed me, François. Next!"

François stared at the judge for a moment, then collected his cake pans and slunk back to his station.

"Our turn." James picked up their cake and headed for Truffleman's table. Alice followed, knees trembling, trying to ignore the cameras.

"I hope I won't be eating eggshells," Truffleman said as he cut himself a slice and lifted it off the plate.

Alice cringed. She'd forgotten about the eggshells.

He took a tiny bite, swallowed, then set down his fork. "It's all right," he said. "I've had better and I've had worse. The top layer is thicker than the bottom — that's a bit sloppy." He looked at the cake again. "Is that supposed to be a crown?"

They nodded. "That was Alice's idea," said James. "It's a nod to Queen Vic —"

"That's fine." Truffleman shrugged. "Next!"

And suddenly, Alice was back in Ms. Kostyniuk's class, sent back to her seat with a giant bowl of rice pudding that no one wanted. All the time and effort they'd spent making their sponge cake — a perfectly good sponge cake — didn't matter one bit.

"Thank you, Tom," James said politely. Alice managed a nod in the judge's direction, but she couldn't look him in the eye.

The winners that day were Sven and Samir, whose cake was deemed "quite edible." They got extra points for decorating it with swirls of icing and raspberry jam, which did look nice, though Alice thought her crown was more interesting.

"And the loser . . ." Miranda paused for an excessively long time. "Is François. François, your cake wasn't baked," she said unnecessarily. "You will not be returning to the Great Hall for another combat. You must leave immediately."

Alice sucked in her breath. Mei-Ling Wu would have never told anyone to leave immediately. Mei-Ling would have given François a big hug and told him he'd tried his best. Alice was tempted to do it herself as she watched the man remove his apron, wave goodbye to the other contestants and leave the Great Hall.

"As for the rest of you," Miranda said, turning to face the remaining contestants, "you've lived to fight another day. We'll see you again next time." She tossed her ponytail and gave the nearest camera a huge smile.

"And that's a wrap!" Jasmina called. "Nice work, everyone!"

The contestants collapsed onto their countertops with a collective groan.

"We did it, sous-chef!" James patted Alice's back. "We passed our first challenge! Can you believe it?"

She couldn't. She couldn't believe it was over, and she couldn't believe they were still in the competition. Nor could she believe how tired she was — she felt as if she'd just run a marathon.

But mostly, she couldn't believe — and she didn't even want to consider — that they had to do it all again, in two days' time.

CHAPTER

7

I t was almost noon by the time the competitors straggled out of the Great Hall, looking (appropriately) as if they'd been through a great battle. Samir and Sven's neckties were askew. Phyllis's blazer was dusted in flour. James had bits of cake batter in his hair.

Alice suspected that she looked as bad if not worse, but she was too tired to care. She dawdled behind the others, half listening as the twins fretted about Diana and François, both of whom had disappeared immediately after the challenge ended.

"We should go look for them," said Toni. "Maybe they want company."

"Or maybe they just want to be alone," said Sven.

Alice could understand that — she couldn't wait to retreat to her father's room and debrief with him about everything that had happened. And after that, they would have a serious talk about escaping before the next challenge began. Maybe Hana would drive them back to the city that very night, or at least drop them off at the nearest bus station.

The more Alice thought about that second option, the more it appealed. They'd simply head home by themselves. Maybe they wouldn't even tell Hana! That seemed reasonable, considering the mess she'd gotten them into.

She tried to get James's attention and signal that it was time to go, but he was chatting with the others and didn't notice.

"Remember what Truffleman said about Phyllis's jam?" Toni chuckled.

Phyllis rolled her eyes. "How was I supposed to know he hates seeds in his jam?"

"*Seeds are one of my greatest pet peeves!*" Samir growled, Truffleman-like.

They all burst out laughing.

"You have to admit, it's pretty exciting to be on a Tom Truffleman show," said Tina.

"If by 'exciting' you mean torturous, then sure," her sister returned.

Alice thought that *torturous* was an excellent word for what they'd just been through. She tried again to catch her father's eye, but again he didn't notice.

"Fun fact about Miranda Summers." Samir lowered his voice. "She's famous for sabotaging another contestant on *Eligible* by putting chewing gum in her hairbrush! The poor girl had to cut it out of her hair right before her date with the eligible guy."

Everyone gasped. "No! Really?" Even James looked riveted, which irritated Alice immensely. *Eligible* sounded even more stupid than she'd thought.

"Miranda got sent home early in the season," Samir went on. "And it was a good thing, too, because the guy they were all competing for later admitted that he wasn't the heir to the world's biggest diamond fortune, like he'd claimed to be. He was a total fraud! Not that I watch the show or anything," he added with a wink.

Alice watched them all laughing, leaning into each other. Just a few hours before, they'd been complete strangers, and now they seemed like best friends. *So much for the combat,* she thought, watching them walk away.

She hung back, feeling suddenly alone. She wasn't like the rest of them: she was the only kid, aside from Diana, who wasn't really a kid and didn't seem interested in making friends.

If Mei-Ling were here, she'd be my friend, Alice thought. Then she pushed that thought away, because it was just too depressing.

She considered going back to their room, then remembered that she hadn't brought a key. So she headed for the lobby, hoping to find a quiet place to sit until James remembered she existed. Thankfully, the lobby was still fairly empty, except for a woman playing the piano, a couple chatting near the door and a boy sitting near the fireplace with a notebook in his lap.

Watching Alice intently.

She did a double-take, startled by the boy's unblinking gaze and big, black eyes. She stared back until he finally looked down at his notebook. Then he took out a pen and began to write.

She squinted, trying to make out what he was writing. But he snaked an arm around the notebook, shielding it.

Now she was *extremely* curious. But before she could move closer, she heard a strange, rumbling noise, like a storm approaching, or a distant parade. She looked around the hall. The boy looked up from his book.

All of a sudden, the festival guests were upon them: dozens of them, stampeding into the lobby dressed in ribbons and frills, bonnets and bow ties, feathered fascinators and top hats. They rustled and hustled across the lobby, chatting and laughing — a few were even dancing! Alice lost sight of the boy as she tucked herself into a corner and waited for the strange parade to pass. Where were they going? And who *were* they?

The crowd had begun to thin when her father found her. "There you are!" he cried. "There's a gathering in the ballroom to kick off the festival. Come on, it's just about to start!"

Kicking off a Victorian festival with a horde of exuberant adults was the last thing Alice wanted to do. She looked back toward the fireplace. The boy with the notebook had disappeared.

"Alice? Are you coming?"

"I'm really tired," she began, but James was already drifting away, following the crowd. Alice let out a strangled sigh, then stomped after him.

They caught up with the other competitors at the door to the ballroom and slipped inside to find the guests clustered around Richard Sibley-McFinch.

He stopped mid-sentence when he saw the competitors. "And here they are!" he cried. The guests spun around and began to applaud. "I was just telling everyone about this morning's big reveal. I'm so glad I don't have to keep quiet about it anymore!

"It was a surprise to me too," he explained once the applause had died down. "Until a few weeks ago, I thought we were hosting *Culinary Chronicles*. I'd heard that the producers were looking for a venue, and I thought it would be a fun addition to our little festival. Of course, I thought it would be a much smaller production, much less stressful." He laughed, a little too loudly. "But I'm thrilled to be hosting a Tom Truffleman show. So thrilled that I haven't slept in a week!"

The crowd laughed, but Alice wasn't sure he was joking.

"Can we watch the competition?" someone asked.

Richard shook his head. "There's no room for us all in the Great Hall. But you'll undoubtedly see the camera crew around — they'll be filming the manor and maybe even parts of the festival. Who knows — you might have a cameo on the show!"

The crowd murmured excitedly.

"Now, I'm sure you're wondering who won the first challenge," he went on. "The good news is that the show's producers decided not to keep this information from you. However, they don't want the public finding out until the show airs in the fall. So, when you return to your rooms, you'll find an agreement to sign, promising you won't tell anyone outside of Gladstone Manor."

The crowd murmured again, less excitedly this time.

"*And*," Richard added, "you'll all be present when Tom Truffleman announces the winner of *Culinary Combat*. This will take place at the big feast on our last night of the festival!"

The guests brightened at the news. They cheered when Richard announced that Sven and Samir had won the first challenge.

"Who lost?" someone asked.

"François," Richard said with a frown. "And sadly, he's already left. He said he plans to hop the first plane to Belize and get some well-deserved rest."

Alice imagined François boarding a plane in his pink flamingo shirt and flying far, far away from *Culinary Combat*. She sighed with envy.

Richard went on to tell the guests about all the activities he'd planned for the week. They would try on Victorian costumes, take dancing lessons, play parlor games, ride horses, learn to cook from Victorian recipes and debate Victorian politics. And there were strange-sounding activities too, like a workshop where people could learn to commune with the dead and another where they would make jewelry with human hair.

Alice looked at James, wondering if she'd heard correctly or if she'd begun to hallucinate from exhaustion. But he was chuckling with Samir and didn't notice her.

She tried to tune back in, but she could barely hear Richard over the guests' chatter.

Who *were* these people? she wondered again, watching them wiggle and bounce in their uncomfortable-looking costumes. Had they actually taken time off work for a Victorian festival? She shook her head, mystified. Then she caught sight of some familiar hair, the color of a red velvet cake. Octavia Sapphire was standing beside her parents, wearing shorts and a T-shirt and looking completely relaxed, as if this were a perfectly normal place to spend a week of her summer vacation.

What is she doing here?

As if she could hear Alice's thoughts, Octavia suddenly turned to look directly at her. Alice immediately dropped her gaze to the floor. Then she turned to her father, to tell him that now it was *definitely* time to go. She couldn't last another minute.

But then Hana appeared, breathless and bright-eyed. "You guys!" she squealed. "I couldn't believe it when I heard the news! Tom *Truffleman!*"

"I know, right?" James grinned, as if he'd actually known who Tom Truffleman was before eight o'clock that morning. "It was wild, Hana. We have so much to tell you!"

We sure do, Alice wanted to say. *Like how this mess is all your fault.*

"It was an experience we'll never forget, wasn't it, Alice?"

"It was pretty terrible," she said. Neither seemed to hear.

"But we prevailed," James assured Hana, who sighed with relief. "We lived to fight another day, as the new host said. What's her name again, Alice?"

Alice shrugged. What did it matter?

"It's just incredible!" Hana squeezed James's hand. "Think of how many people will see you cooking! It's such great exposure for you."

"Exposure?" Alice repeated, but the crowd started cheering again, and no one heard her. Since when did they want exposure? Did Hana even *know* them?

"Go forth and be festive, everyone!" Richard cried. "Have a spectacular first day at the festival!"

The guests applauded one final time, then made a beeline for the door. Alice tucked herself behind her father to avoid getting trampled.

"What shall we do now?" James asked. "Costume fittings? Etiquette lessons? Just kidding, Alice." He patted her head, as if she were five years old. "How about lunch?"

"Lunch sounds great," Hana chirped.

"I don't really —" Alice began.

"Oh, let's invite the other contestants too. You'll really like them, Hana."

And before Alice could protest — vehemently this time — they swept her off to lunch with a crowd.

By the time they returned to their room, it was mid-afternoon. Alice staggered to her bed and collapsed facedown on the pillows.

"You okay, sous-chef?" James kicked off his shoes. "It's been quite the day, hasn't it?"

"Yes." She rolled onto her back with a moan. "And I don't think I can do it again."

"What do you mean? We did a great job!"

She sifted through the day's events, recalling how she'd frozen at the beginning of the challenge, how she'd dropped a broken egg into their mixing bowl, and how she'd stood before Tom Truffleman as he sniffed at their "sloppy" sponge cake. RealiTV viewers would see all of it.

She sat up on the bed. "We should get out while we still can."

"Get out?" He scratched his head, discovering a dollop of cake batter. "You don't mean we should leave, do you?"

"That's exactly what I mean."

"Oh, sous-chef. I know it wasn't fun for you, especially with all those cameras around, but you did really well. And what's more, I'm certain it's going to get better."

She flopped back onto the pillows with a groan. "You don't know that."

"Well no, but at least now we know what to expect. There'll be no more surprises. And just imagine — if we win this competition, we'll get our own cookbook! Wouldn't that be amazing?"

"We're *not* going to write a cookbook," Alice said to the ceiling.

"But imagine if we did! What would it be called?" he mused. "Let's see . . . *James and Alice's* . . ."

"*Recipes for Disaster*," she grumbled.

He chuckled. "That's pretty good. Now look, why don't you get some rest — it's been a long day. I'm going to go practice knotting my lucky scarf." He wandered off to the bathroom.

"I don't need rest," Alice grumped. She pulled her phone out, tapped open her PHOMO app and found two new photos from Mat. The first showed a diorama he'd made at camp: a jungle scene, complete with jaguars sculpted from clay. The second showed him with a big group of kids. They had their arms slung around each other and were laughing at the camera, clearly having the time of their lives.

The sight made Alice's chest hurt, and she desperately wished she were back at home. Or anywhere, really — just not at Gladstone Manor. She imagined herself on a flight to Belize, although she wasn't even sure where that was.

She switched off her phone and tucked it away, wishing they'd never come.

CHAPTER 8

A lice spent the rest of the day moping in their room, emerging only for dinner, where she nearly fell asleep in her soup while James and Hana chattered on about the sessions they couldn't wait to attend the following day. Afterwards, they wanted to go listen to music in the parlor, but Alice insisted she was too tired. She was almost too tired to care when they went without her.

She was still feeling groggy the next morning at breakfast when James announced that he was going to a lecture on Victorian cutlery and serving utensils.

"Every object on the Victorian table had a very specific use," he explained to Alice. "Like grape scissors and ice cream forks and mustache cups."

"Mustache cups?" Alice inched her chair closer to their table so that two women in big, bell-shaped skirts could pass. Unlike the previous morning, they were now surrounded by festival guests loading up on ham and eggs and chattering about the day ahead. Their incessant buzz was making Alice's head hurt.

Her only consolation was that it was a rest day, which meant she wouldn't have to cook.

She couldn't remember a time when she hadn't wanted to cook.

"Have I not told you about mustache cups?" James looked incredulous. "Well! They were invented to help Victorian men drink tea. You see, back then men waxed their mustaches to hold the hairs in place. But if they drank tea, the wax would melt and the mustache would droop — a real embarrassment. So someone invented a teacup with a lip to protect the mustache. Ingenious, right?"

"Weird." Alice sipped her orange juice.

"Am I sensing you don't want to come?"

She shook her head.

"But what will you do? You'll have the whole day to yourself."

She wasn't sure, but she suspected it would involve hiding in their room, scrolling through PHOMO and imagining herself elsewhere.

"All right." He took one last gulp of tea and stood up. "I should go. The lecture starts in five minutes. But if you need anything, you can text me."

This made her laugh. "You don't text!" In fact, he rarely even turned his cell phone on.

He looked insulted. "I do! Hana taught me."

Hana. Of course. Alice tried not to roll her eyes.

He kissed her forehead and left the dining room. And once again Alice was on her own, with a full day ahead of her and nothing to do. She sighed, finished her orange juice and stood to go.

"Alice? It's Alice, right?"

She jumped at the sight of Octavia Sapphire. Beside her stood a dark-eyed boy whom Alice recognized immediately. It was the boy with the notebook.

"Alice?" Octavia cocked her head to one side. Her hair cascaded over her shoulder like a red-velvet waterfall.

"Um, yes. I'm Alice." She tried to focus on Octavia's face instead of her hair. "How did you know?"

"I asked Richard." Octavia extended a hand for Alice to shake. "I'm Tavi. We were going to be roommates, you know."

"Yes," Alice said, noting that Octavia — *Tavi* — had a very firm handshake. It was the kind of handshake you expected from an adult, not a kid. She tried to think of something else to say but couldn't come up with anything.

"There's loads of space in my room if you ever change your mind or just want to visit," Tavi told her. "There's an *actual* fireplace — it's super cool. I mean, we're not allowed to light it, but last night I borrowed my dad's tablet and found a fireplace video, and I set it up where the real fire would have been! It was super cozy."

"Wow." Alice would never have thought of making a virtual fire.

The notebook boy sighed loudly. "It's starting in five minutes," he said. "We have to go."

"Oh, yeah. Want to come with us?" asked Tavi.

"To learn about cutlery?" Alice wrinkled her nose.

Tavi laughed. "No! We're going to . . . What's it called again?"

"Bartitsu," the boy said, as if he'd told her a hundred times already.

"What's that?" asked Alice.

"You don't know?" The boy's eyes widened.

She shook her head.

"It's a Victorian martial art," he said.

"We're going to learn to fight like Victorian gentlemen, using umbrellas or something." Tavi shrugged. "I'm not really sure, but it sounds better than the dance lesson my parents went to. Or that cutlery thing."

"Sherlock Holmes used to practice Bartitsu," the boy informed Alice. "You *do* know who Sherlock Holmes is, don't you?"

"Of course," Alice said, not liking his tone.

"Great, let's go!" Tavi ushered them toward the door. "It's in Room 313, which sounds super unlucky. Maybe we'll see some ghosts. This place must be crawling with them!" She marched them across the lobby and over to the staircase, and Alice followed, wondering what she'd gotten herself into.

"What's your name?" she asked the boy as they climbed the stairs to the third floor.

"Henry," he said. "Henry Oh."

"I'm Alice Fleck."

"I know," he said. "You're part of *Culinary Combat*."

"How did you know?"

"I found out," he replied simply, and Alice recalled him scribbling in his notebook the previous day. Had he been writing about her?

"But you didn't win," he added matter-of-factly.

"Well, no," she said, now disliking his tone very much. "But we didn't lose, either."

"Oh, I know. The guy who lost forgot to turn on his oven." Henry raised an eyebrow. "Or did he?"

Alice paused at the top of the stairs. "What are you talking about?"

He shrugged. "Just a theory I'm working on. Look, here's our room." He stepped inside before Alice could ask what he meant.

"Henry has a lot of theories." Tavi nudged her through the door. "He wants to be a detective."

"I'm already a detective!" Henry called back.

Tavi grinned. "Come on, let's go fight some Victorian gentlemen."

Room 313 was like no room Alice had seen at Gladstone Manor. It had no chandelier, no velvet sofas, no fireplace. In fact, it had no furniture at all, just gymnasium-style mats spread out on the floor. Seven adults were already sitting on the mats, and Henry and Tavi marched over to join them. But Alice hung back, suddenly struck by the fact that she was walking into an *actual martial arts class.*

She recalled a time, earlier that year, when Cami Diaz had decided to teach Mat some jiu-jitsu moves. They would, she'd said, help him survive middle school, where anything could happen. Mat had ended up with a sprained wrist and a bloody nose.

Before she could turn back, Hana hopped up from the floor, wearing a T-shirt and jogging pants. "Alice! You came!"

Alice's stomach sank. "Oh, hi," she said. "You're learning this . . . martial arts thing too?"

"Nope." Hana grinned. "I'm teaching it."

Alice was startled. "You *are*?"

"You *are*?" echoed Henry.

"I am." Hana turned to him. "Why wouldn't I be?"

"No reason," he said quickly. He sat down at her feet and pulled out his notebook.

She turned back to Alice. "Don't you remember? I told you guys all about it in the car. My grandfather was a sensei who taught jujutsu in Japan, the original Japanese form of Brazilian jiu-jitsu — he's been my inspiration since I was a kid."

Alice did not remember this at all, but then, she had tuned Hana out to focus on PHOMO.

"Come in, come in!" Hana called to a couple hovering at the door. "Take a seat on the floor. Unless you're in costume — then grab a chair." She waved at a woman wearing a dress that looked a bit like a doily on a dinner table.

Henry spun to face Alice as soon as she sat down. "You know the teacher?"

Alice nodded. "She's my dad's, um, girlfriend."

"Wow," Henry breathed.

Alice pursed her lips but said nothing.

"All right, let's get started!" Hana clapped her hands for attention. "I'm so glad you all came today. My name is Hana Holmes."

"Holmes," Henry whispered reverently. "That's so cool."

"I'm a historian," Hana went on. "I study Victorian times, especially the suffragette movement. And it was the suffragettes who brought me to Bartitsu. For those of you who've never heard of it, Bartitsu was a martial art practiced mainly by Victorian gentlemen. But some suffragettes practiced it too, since they needed to protect themselves from people who didn't believe they should have the right to vote. And sometimes those people got violent."

Tavi muttered something about those people being complete idiots.

"The word *Bartitsu* is a combination of the name Barton — that's the guy who invented it — and jiu-jitsu, or the Japanese jujutsu." Hana told them. "It involves moves from those disciplines and other martial arts, but it also makes use of objects that a Victorian might have had on hand if they were, say, out for a stroll and just happened to get attacked by ruffians. Any idea what they might have used?"

Henry's hand shot up. "An umbrella or a walking stick."

"Very good," said Hana. "You must be familiar with Bartitsu."

He nodded vigorously.

Alice suddenly recalled the three umbrellas in the back of Hana's car. She'd brought them not for rain or for shading herself from the sun, but for *fighting Victorian ruffians*! "Whoa," she whispered, wondering how her father had neglected to mention this weird hobby of Hana's.

"We'll start with a demonstration. Leo?" Hana nodded at a young man, who hopped to his feet. "Leo and I studied Bartitsu together for years. So don't worry: no matter what it looks like, no one is going to get hurt. Right, Leo?"

"Hopefully not!" He grinned.

Henry leaned forward, notebook and pen at the ready.

Hana began by strolling across the room, carrying a closed umbrella like a walking stick. She seemed unaware of Leo lurking not far behind her until he lunged to attack. In a flash, she seized her umbrella in both hands and lifted it to block his arm. Then she twisted it to the right and down. Leo started to fall, and in one swift motion she brought the handle of her umbrella down on top of him, knocking him flat to the floor.

Everyone gasped. Henry scribbled notes furiously. Alice felt as if she too had been knocked down flat. Who *was* Hana Holmes?!

"I'm okay!" Leo assured them, hopping to his feet. "One of the first things we learned is how to fall without getting hurt. We did get a lot of bruises in practice, though."

"One more time?" Hana said. He nodded.

This time, they each grabbed a cane and began walking toward each other from opposite sides of the room. When he was an arm's length away from Hana, Leo lifted his cane to hit her. But Hana was faster: she swung her cane above her head and brought it down square on his shoulder. Then, while Leo reeled from the blow, she grabbed his leg with the hook of her cane and sent him tumbling backward onto a mat.

Alice flinched. Henry gasped. Tavi cried, "Amazing!"

The class applauded, and Alice joined in. She would never have guessed Hana was capable of *that*.

"I'll teach you a few basic moves today," Hana said. "And in our next session, tomorrow afternoon, we might start sparring. Everyone ready?"

"Yes!" Henry practically shrieked, already on his feet.

She handed them each a weapon — Alice received a sturdy black umbrella — then showed them how to lunge at an imaginary opponent and jab them with the tip.

Alice stood between Henry and Tavi to practice. Henry was all business, eyes narrowed and jaw clenched. Tavi looked less intense but had more panache — she moved like a dancer, or maybe a fencer.

"I took some sword-fighting classes once," she explained when she saw Alice watching her.

"Sword fighting?" Alice nearly dropped her umbrella.

"At a medieval reenactment camp," Tavi said casually, stabbing her imaginary opponent in the chest.

"Medieval reenactment camp?"

Tavi nodded. "My parents are historical reenactment fanatics. We go to at least one festival or camp every year. We've done medieval times, the Tudor era . . . we even did a Roaring Twenties dance camp and learned the Charleston." She tapped her feet.

Alice tried to process this. "So do you . . . *like* . . . these reenactment things?"

"Oh yeah, they're pretty fun," said Tavi. "And I think this one will be great. I love the Victorians — they were super into ghosts, and I am too."

"Huh." Alice would never have pegged Octavia Sapphire for a ghost-loving historical reenactment fan. She wanted to ask whether Tavi actually told people about her unusual interests, but she decided it was too soon for such a question.

"Have you ever been to something like this before?" Tavi asked.

Alice shook her head. "I'm just here for *Culinary Chron* — I mean, *Combat*."

"It's Henry's first festival too," said Tavi. "My parents are friends with his mom, so we took him with us while she went to a yoga retreat. I think he likes it so far." She grinned at Henry, who was muttering "Take that!" as he pierced the air with his umbrella.

"Tell me about *Culinary Combat*," Tavi said as they began to practice again. "You thought you were going to be on that other show, right? What was it called?"

"*Culinary Chronicles*."

"Were you a big fan?"

Alice hesitated. "I watched it sometimes," she said carefully. "I liked the host."

"And now you're stuck with Tom Truffleman." Tavi grimaced. "I've seen him on TV — he's kind of scary."

"*Super* scary," Alice agreed, glad she understood.

"So how'd you get on the show? Do you cook a lot? Tell me all about it," said Tavi.

Alice bit her lip. Not since the calf-boiling incident had she told anyone her age about her hobby. But Tavi had just admitted to taking sword-fighting classes and going to historical re-enactment festivals, and she hadn't even seemed embarrassed about it.

Still, Alice hesitated.

"Henry told me what happened with François and his oven," Tavi added. "Sounds dramatic."

Alice recalled what Henry had said as they were climbing the stairs. "How did Henry find out?"

"He overheard the production crew talking about it yesterday. You can't keep anything from Henry, you know. He's an expert eavesdropper and a first-class snoop."

"I'm not a snoop," Henry called. "I'm a detective!"

"See?" said Tavi. "Anyway, no pressure. But if you feel like talking about it, you can." She leaned on her cane and waited.

To her great surprise, Alice *did* feel like talking about it. She felt the story bubbling inside her like soup on a stovetop, and her longing to share it was suddenly stronger than her fear of the consequences. So she gripped her umbrella in both hands, took a breath and began to tell Tavi everything.

She told her about the big surprise, the first cooking challenge, the fierce judge and the disappointing new host. She told her how Tom Truffleman had almost refused to let her cook because she was a kid. She even admitted to shattering an egg and nearly ruining their sponge cake.

And Tavi Sapphire, with her red-velvet hair and casual confidence, did not make fun of Alice — not even once, not even an eye roll. Neither did Henry, who was almost definitely eavesdropping while he lunged and jabbed beside them.

It was such a relief, she nearly cried.

"That sounds *insane*," Tavi said once she had finished. "And you have to do it all again tomorrow?"

Alice nodded. There was little hope now of convincing her father that they should escape.

Tavi shook her head. "I've never seen *Culinary Chronicles*. But I'm kind of obsessed with this show called *Desserts to Die For*. Have you seen it?"

Alice hadn't.

"It's like a cooking show, but the chefs make creepy recipes, like desserts that have killed people, desserts served at funerals, the last desserts people ate before they died — that kind of thing. Did you know there's a town in Switzerland where everyone used to spend their lives aging cheese to be eaten at their own funerals?"

Alice did not. Nor would she have expected Tavi to be so enthused about it.

Clearly, Octavia Sapphire was full of surprises.

And so was Hana Holmes, who was now announcing that the session was already over. Alice couldn't believe the time had passed so quickly — and that she'd actually enjoyed it.

"Our next session is tomorrow at one o'clock," Hana said as she collected everyone's weapons. "Hope to see you all there!" She paused in front of Alice and raised her eyebrows.

Alice considered it. She hadn't gotten hurt or embarrassed herself, and she might even have made a new friend. All in all, it had gone remarkably well.

Still, she didn't want to make any promises. Especially to Hana.

"Maybe," she said. "I'll see."

CHAPTER
9

The Bartitsu lesson helped Alice keep her mind off *Culinary Combat* for the rest of the day, most of which she spent reading cookbooks and scrolling through PHOMO. But by dinnertime, all she could think about was the next morning's challenge. It loomed like a shadow over the dinner table, where James told her all about the specialized dining implements he'd learned about, like celery vases and snail forks. It followed her to bed and tapped at her shoulder while she was trying to fall asleep.

When the alarm went off at seven o'clock the next morning, she was already trembling.

They dressed quickly and quietly and headed downstairs for breakfast, but Alice couldn't manage even a bite of her croissant.

"You have to eat something," James insisted, but it was no use. She was certain she wouldn't be able to eat until it was over.

They gathered with the other competitors outside the doors of the Great Hall. Sven and Samir looked dapper, as usual, this time in yellow-and-green-striped bow ties. The twins were still wearing their matching cupcake sweatshirts — the producers, they explained, had insisted on it.

"They want us to play up the fact that we're twins," Toni explained. "But they want Tina to be the kind, sweet twin, and me to be the twin with attitude." She rolled her eyes.

"They asked me to act goofier." Samir grinned. "I think because Sven is so serious." He poked his partner in the ribs. Sven shook his head but chuckled.

"They asked me if I'd faint again," Diana admitted softly. "They said it's good to have someone panicking on set."

Toni harrumphed. "That's ridiculous!"

Alice nodded, wondering if the producers would ask her to act a certain way too. She hoped not — it was hard enough just being herself.

She sighed heavily as they filed into the hall, and her father squeezed her shoulder.

"What do you think we'll be making today?" he asked cheerfully. "I'm betting on mincemeat, or maybe a — Oh!" He ground to a halt alongside the others. "What happened?"

Five workstations now stood before them, down from the original six. But that wasn't the biggest change: somehow, the workstations had *shrunk*! Each one was missing at least four feet of counter space, and they'd been squished together, leaving little room to move in between.

"It was Tom's idea," Jasmina explained, hustling over. "He thought that shrinking the stations would make the challenge more difficult."

"We'll all have less space to work in," Phyllis observed. "But the pairs will be at a serious disadvantage."

"He probably wants us to start fighting over space," Toni grumbled. "That's just mean."

"This station is tiny," Sven fretted. "Our kitchen at home is four times as big!"

"We'll just have to be very organized," Samir told him. "No making messes."

"I never make messes!" Sven snapped.

Alice looked at her father, eyebrows raised. Tom Truffleman's plan was working already.

The door banged open and the judge himself marched in. "Makeup!" he yelled. "I need makeup!"

"Here we go," Jasmina sighed as the makeup crew scurried over. "What's up, Tom?"

"I had a terrible sleep last night!" he proclaimed. "Just awful."

"Is it the pillows again?"

"Yes, it's the pillows again!" he stormed. "I asked for *fluffy* pillows and I got *flat* ones! I can't sleep with flat pillows!"

"Ask Richard to send up some fluffy pillows," Jasmina murmured to a member of the cleaning crew, who took off at a sprint.

Alice watched the judge with a growing sense of dread. Now they had tiny workstations *and* an ill-tempered judge to contend with, on top of everything else.

"We'll do our best, Tom," Jasmina promised. "Now, where's Miranda? Has anyone seen her? We have to start filming in ten minutes."

"I'm here!" The host hurried through the door. "Sorry I'm late. I got up super early and drove to the spa down the road to get a manicure. Cute, right?" She showed Jasmina her pearly-pink nails. "And then of course I had to do a quick photo shoot for my PHOMO followers. But I'm here now! Camera ready!"

"I'm so glad," Jasmina said through clenched teeth. "We're starting in eight minutes."

Miranda took her place in front of the cameras, still admiring her manicure. "Hey, can I hold something?" she asked Jasmina. "So that the camera can catch my nails?"

"No." Jasmina sounded as flat as Tom's pillow. "Everyone, go to your stations and get ready!"

The crew dashed around, clipping microphones to collars, straightening aprons and spritzing flyaways. Then the countdown began, and once again, Alice could only brace herself for what was to come and hope it wouldn't be too awful.

"Today's challenge won't be as easy as the last," Miranda warned them once she'd finished her introduction. "It's going to test all your skills, and at least one of you will be forced to leave the Great Hall, like François. I hear he's on a beach in Belize now, which sounds pretty good to me!" She laughed and waved her hands in the air. Alice guessed she meant to show off her nails, but it looked as if she was being swarmed by bees.

"You guys will wish you were on a beach too when you find out what you're making today. Ready to hear about it?"

The competitors held their breath.

"You've got three hours to put your own creative spin on a Victorian jelly dessert! There's a basic recipe in the top drawer of your station, but you'll have to decide on the color, flavor and shape. Everything you'll need is on the shelves or in the fridge. Anything to add, Tom?"

The judge nodded. "At the last challenge, you proved yourselves capable of making a very simple cake — some of you, anyway. But today, I want to see you take risks. I want jelly desserts to remember, and I do not under any circumstances want to be bored."

"No boring jelly desserts!" Miranda chanted. "Get going, everyone!"

Alice spun to face her father, filled with dread. "Dad," she whispered, "please tell me we don't have to make the gelatin ourselves. Please tell me I don't have to boil calves' feet on TV. Because if I have to do that, I will die."

On cue, a video camera popped up beside her. Alice fought the urge to shove it away.

"Let's check the recipe." James pulled it out of the drawer and looked it over while Alice tried to turn away from the camera. "It calls for leaves of gelatin, pre-prepared."

She nearly collapsed with relief.

"It's a very basic recipe," he went on. "We'll have to make a lot of decisions ourselves. Oh, how about we make blanc-mange?"

"No." Alice straightened, suddenly energized by the fact that she wouldn't have to make gelatin. "We have to take risks, remember? Blancmange is too boring."

"I'd say it's elegant in its simplicity," insisted James.

"Nuh-uh." She shook her head. "We need something interesting. Something memorable." She thought about the jelly desserts in *The Victorian Cooking Compendium*: there was one in the shape of a lion, another that looked like a cathedral and even one that looked like a plate of bacon and eggs.

"Let's see what kinds of molds they have." James pointed to the shelves, where the other competitors were already huddled.

"Good idea," said Alice.

On their way to the shelves, they passed Diana, who was sprinting back to her workstation with two pints of strawberries, looking as if she'd just robbed a bank. Over near the fridges, Sven and Samir were having a heated argument over a bottle of orange cordial. Phyllis, however, looked perfectly peaceful as she plucked ingredients off the shelves.

"I'm making blancmange," she told them. "It's my very favorite."

"See?" James hissed, but Alice shook her head. They had to do better.

Most of the competitors had chosen dome- or ring-shaped molds. This, Alice knew, was a safe choice; it was much easier to remove a jelly dessert from a mold shaped like a dome than one shaped like a lion. But it wasn't nearly as interesting. She began to search the shelves for the perfect shape.

"What about these?" She held up a set of six brass spheres, each about the size of an orange. "I think I've seen them in a cookbook. You pour the liquid into the spout, and when it's set, you take them apart using this clasp." She demonstrated; the sphere opened neatly into two halves.

James crouched beside her to examine them. "These are beautiful antiques."

"We could make an entire set, each one a different color!" She could see it in her mind's eye and was itching to try it.

"It sounds like a lot of work," said James. "But I guess if you think so —"

"I do!" She hopped up, molds in hand. "Let's go!"

They gathered sugar, gelatin and an assortment of fruit, then hurried back to their station. A camera followed as usual, but Alice tried her best to ignore it and focus on the task at hand. They had a lot of work to do, and less than three hours to do it.

Making a jelly dessert wasn't as easy as making a sponge cake, but it wasn't that hard, either. They soaked some leaves of gelatin in cold water to soften them, then put a pot of water on the stove. Once it was boiling, they would toss in some sugar and stir it until it dissolved, then take the pot off the stove and add the gelatin.

When the water began to bubble, Alice measured out her sugar. She was about to dump it into the pot when her father stopped her.

"Wait. Are you sure that's sugar?"

Alice blinked at him. "What else would it be?"

"The jar isn't labeled," he pointed out. "Did you check?"

She shook her head — she'd just grabbed it from the shelf. Her father dipped a spoon into the jar, then tasted it. "Definitely salt."

"No!" She nearly fainted. "That would have been a total disaster!"

He agreed. "But it wasn't. Let's just check first, okay?"

First eggshells, and now salt instead of sugar. "I almost ruined everything! Again!"

"You didn't," James assured her. "Now, you stay here, and I'll go find the real sugar." He raced off, leaving her clinging to the counter.

"You all right, Alice?" Toni called from across the aisle. "You look pale."

"I'm fine." She closed her eyes, took a deep breath and tried to convince herself it was all okay.

When she opened her eyes again, Tom Truffleman was standing nearby, staring at her. Meg stood beside him with her video camera.

"Oh!" Alice gasped.

The judge pursed his lips. "Alice, right?"

"Mm-hm." She tucked her hands into her apron pockets so the camera wouldn't catch them shaking.

"Where's your father?"

She pointed toward the shelves, where James stood with his back to them. She would have to face Tom Truffleman alone.

86

He surveyed their ingredients. "What has James decided to make?"

"We're, um, making sphere-shaped jellies. In these." She held up one of the molds. "Each one will be a different color and flavor, hopefully. I mean definitely," she added quickly. "Yes. Definitely."

"Ambitious." Tom picked up one of the brass spheres to examine it. "Has James ever used these before?"

"No," Alice admitted. "But I think I know how."

He raised an eyebrow. "And how would you know?"

"I read about it once," she said. "In a cookbook."

He snickered. "And you think that's good enough?"

Alice opened her mouth to reply, then shut it, because clearly he meant that it wasn't good enough. And maybe even that *she* wasn't good enough. She felt herself shrivel inside, like a grape left in the sun.

Across the aisle, Tina tsked. "That's not nice."

It wasn't nice, Alice agreed. Nor was it fair. She had a good idea and was trying her best, and stupid Tom Truffleman had interrupted to make her feel terrible. Inside her apron pockets, her hands balled into fists.

"I've made jellies before — a lot of them," she informed him. "It isn't that hard, especially when you don't have to make the gelatin yourself. You don't even have to think about where it came from."

Meg chuckled quietly behind her camera.

Truffleman's eyes widened, then narrowed. "Is that so? Then tell me —" He broke off when James appeared with a jar of sugar.

"Got it!" he puffed. "Crisis averted."

"Crisis?" Truffleman spun toward him. "What now?"

"We almost had a mix-up, but we caught it just in time," James assured him. "All good now."

"I see." The judge looked disappointed. "You've got a complicated project here, James."

"We do," he agreed. "And, to be honest, it was Alice's idea. If it turns out, she'll get the credit."

Truffleman glanced at Alice as if she were a speck of mold on a block of cheese. Then he turned and walked away.

Meg lowered her camera. "Ignore him," she whispered to Alice. "You're doing a great job." Then she hurried after the judge.

"Sorry to leave you alone for that." James set the jar on the counter. "Are you all right?"

Alice took her hands out of her pockets and shook them. She felt hot and prickly, and more determined than ever to show the judge what they were capable of. "I'm fine." She picked up the jar of sugar. "Let's do this."

With six different jellies to make, they had to work quickly. They added the sugar to the water, then separated it into six batches, adding gelatin leaves and a different kind of fruit juice to each one, to make each sphere a different color. Then they carefully poured the liquid into the molds and put them all in a refrigerator.

"Phew," James said after they'd shut the door — very carefully, so as not to jostle anything. "Now we've got an hour and a half to wait and hope they set."

Alice shook her head. "*Now* we have to decide how to display them."

"We could put them on a nice plate?" he suggested.

"And bore Tom Truffleman to tears?"

"Okay, okay. Do you have something in mind?"

She did. It had come to her while she was filling the spheres, which reminded her of the time she and Mat had made papier-mâché planets for a diorama of the galaxy. "I think we should make them look like planets."

"Planets!"

"Try to picture it," she said. "We'll find a dark background, like a plate . . . or a cookie sheet? Then we'll draw a map of the galaxy on it, and we'll put each sphere in the place of a planet." She bit her lip. "What do you think?"

James blinked at her. "Sous-chef!"

"I know it sounds complicated but —"

"It sounds brilliant!" he cried, then lowered his voice. "Did I ever tell you about the Victorian women who mapped the stars?"

"The what?"

"There were many of them, all across the world. You see, at the time women weren't allowed to join most astronomical societies, but they did important behind-the-scenes work that really changed the study of astronomy forever. One in particular —"

"Dad! We need to get started."

"Right," he said. "Tell me what to do."

They spent the next hour mapping the galaxy. First they made a stiff, white icing, which they used to draw circles and lines on a big cookie sheet, depicting the planets' orbits. James tried to model it after an old astronomical map he'd seen at the university. The Victorians, he told Alice, were very into astronomy.

While they worked, he told her about Maria Mitchell, an American girl who at twelve years old had helped her father, an amateur astronomer, calculate the exact moment of a solar eclipse. Later, she went on to discover a comet through her own telescope, but she had to write about it under her father's name, since of course —"

"She was a woman," Alice finished with a sigh.

James nodded. "It took a while, but eventually she won a gold medal for discovering that comet. And she became the first woman elected to the American Academy of Arts and Sciences."

"Hear, hear!" Tina called. Alice hadn't realized the twins were listening, as were Phyllis and Diana, as they waited for their desserts to set.

Sven and Samir, however, were busy decorating a cake stand — and it didn't seem to be going well.

"Could you please watch your elbow?" Sven snapped. "That's the third time you've hit me!"

"There's no room for my elbows, or anything else!" Samir protested. "It's not my fault this station is tiny."

Alice had completely forgotten about the shrunken work-stations — she and James had been managing just fine, and she suddenly realized why. "We're used to this," she said.

"Hmm?"

"It's just like our kitchen in the old apartment. Remember?" That kitchen had been roughly the size of a closet. For nearly ten years they'd slipped and shimmied around each other, passing ingredients and ducking out of each other's way. It had become a familiar dance, and they'd been doing it all morning without thinking.

"You're right." James smiled. "It's second nature for us."

Alice smiled too. Tom Truffleman's attempts to turn part-ners against each other had failed — at least in their case.

"Fifteen minutes left!" called Miranda.

"This is it!" James ran to the fridge to retrieve their molds

90

while Alice filled the sink with hot water. According to *The Victorian Cooking Compendium*, the best way to get jellies out of particularly tricky molds was to submerge them in hot water for a split second before opening them. And hopefully they'd find that the liquid had set — otherwise, they'd have a sticky mess on their hands.

"Want to do the honors?" James asked.

Alice pictured herself dropping a sphere into the sink and ruining everything. She glanced at a nearby videographer, who was probably waiting for a disaster. "Maybe you should."

"I'll do half, and you do half," he decided.

No jellies fell to the bottom of the sink. In fact, they all came out perfectly spherical, beautifully colored and impeccably wobbly. They set each one in place on the map, then stood back to survey their work.

"I think they're wonderful." James squeezed her shoulder. "Don't you?"

Alice nodded, wishing she could take a photo and send it to Mat.

"Time's up!" Miranda waved her hands in the air. "Step away from your desserts and get ready for the judging!"

Sven and Samir went first, with a peach and chartreuse jelly in the shape of a ring. Tom Truffleman poked and prodded it, scooped a spoonful and slurped it up.

"Nice flavors," he decided. "But why would you make something so plain?"

"There's an interesting story behind it!" Samir offered. "This was the dessert served in the first-class dining room of the *Titanic* the night it sank."

Alice shivered at the thought. She wondered if Tavi knew about this from *Desserts to Die For*.

Looking unimpressed, the judge waved them away.

Phyllis's blancmange fared no better. "It's a fine blancmange — pretty near perfect, to be honest," he said. "But is there anything more boring than blancmange?"

"Boring!" Phyllis exclaimed. "Blancmange is a delight! The Victorians certainly thought so!" She looked as if she wanted to overturn the dish on his head.

The twins' dessert was beautiful: filled with berries and shaped like a crown. But the judge poked it just once and declared it too soft. "It needed another half hour in the fridge," he said, refusing even to taste it.

"Why that little —" Toni seethed as he waved them away. Once again, Tina shushed her.

Next came Diana, with a strawberry-filled dessert that wobbled nicely. But when Truffleman tasted it, he gagged. "What on earth?"

Diana paled. "What's wrong?"

"What's wrong?" He spat and sputtered. "This is *salty*, not sweet! Did you actually use salt instead of sugar?"

Alice grabbed James's arm. "She mixed them up too!"

Truffleman shook his head in disgust and waved poor Diana away. Then he motioned for James and Alice to bring up their creation.

"Hmm," he said, surveying their astrological map. "This is different."

Alice crossed her fingers very tightly as he nudged the spheres with a spoon, then sampled each one with his eyes closed.

"The flavors are bold and distinct," he murmured. "And the display . . ." He paused, then opened his eyes. "Well done, James. It's clever and inventive, and it tastes good too."

James's mouth fell open. "Th-thank you, Tom!" he stammered. "Oh, but remember, it was Alice's —"

But the judge was already walking off set to pass his verdict on to Miranda.

"The winners today are James and Alice!" the host announced minutes later. "And the loser is . . . Diana, whose dessert was salty instead of sweet. Diana, you will not be returning to the Great —"

Diana was halfway out the door before she could even finish.

"Oh. Um, okay." Miranda turned back to the remaining contestants. "Well, the rest of you have all lived to fight another day! We'll see you next time on *Culinary Combat*."

"And that is a wrap!" Jasmina called, sounding relieved.

Immediately, a crowd descended on James and Alice's station to admire their creation and congratulate them for earning actual praise from Tom Truffleman, which everyone agreed was practically unheard of. The mood turned celebratory, and the Great Hall grew raucous. Someone popped a bottle of champagne, though it wasn't even lunchtime. Someone else appeared with sandwiches and cookies for everyone.

They didn't emerge from the hall until a half hour later. By that time, Alice's head was spinning.

"Wasn't that incredible?" James ruffled her hair as they headed down the hall toward the lobby. "We knocked Truffleman's socks off! We should be very proud of ourselves, sous-chef."

She nodded. It *had* been incredible. And she *was* proud.

And yet . . . she couldn't shake the feeling that something wasn't right.

"The thing is," she began, not sure how to express it. But before she could try, a familiar voice squealed, "James! Alice! I just heard the news!" They turned to see Hana barreling down the hall toward them.

"You heard already? How did you —" James began, but Hana threw her arms around him and kissed him on the mouth.

And that, after everything else that had happened, was just too much for Alice.

She turned on her heel and ran.

CHAPTER

10

She didn't get far before a herd of festival guests appeared, charging toward the Great Hall.

"Little girl, have you seen Tom Truffleman?" one asked as Alice tried to squeeze between them.

"He's a world-famous judge," another added. "We need his autograph!"

"And selfies!" one giggled.

She pushed through the crowd and resumed her flight. When she reached the lobby, she kept going, dodging more guests posing for photos in front of the fireplace and side-stepping Roslyn the whippet, who was pacing around the room, looking as agitated as Alice felt. She ran up the stairs to the second floor, then down the hallway to their room. Only when she reached it did she realize that, once again, she didn't have a key — she'd given hers to her father for safekeeping when they'd left the room that morning.

"Darn it!" She stamped her foot. Obviously she couldn't go back and ask him for it. He was probably still kissing Hana! She shuddered.

What she needed was a place to sit by herself and think

through everything that had happened. Somewhere quiet, preferably with no one else in it.

Then she remembered the library on the third floor. It was perfect. For someone who wanted to be left alone, there was no place better than a library.

She ran back down the hall and up the stairs to the third floor. She turned right at the landing and flung herself through the doorway, where the library awaited her with its floor-to-ceiling bookshelves, brown leather armchairs —

And Henry Oh, scribbling in his notebook.

"Oh." She ground to a halt.

"Oh." He looked surprised, then disappointed. "Hello."

"Hi," she said, equally unenthused. Where would she go now?

He looked down at his notebook, then back up at her. "Are you going to stay?"

"I'm not sure." She tugged on her braid. "I came here to think."

"Me too," he said, with a look that implied he'd been doing just that until she interrupted him.

She sighed. "I'll go somewhere else."

"No, you can stay," he said reluctantly. "We can both think here, if we're quiet. I need quiet to think."

Alice nodded. She was in no mood for talking. She sat down in the armchair across from Henry's and found it cold and stiff, nothing like the comfy old reading chairs they had at home.

Now more than ever, she missed home.

She told herself she ought to be happy. She'd had a great idea, and it had turned out perfectly. Who cared if stupid Tom Truffleman wouldn't believe she was the one who'd come up with it? That didn't matter.

Did it?

Alice thought about Maria Mitchell, the young astronomer. Was this how she'd felt, publishing her findings under her father's name? That hadn't been fair either.

"What's not fair?" asked Henry.

"What?" Alice hadn't realized she'd said it aloud. "Oh. Nothing."

He watched her for a moment, then said, "You won the challenge today."

Her mouth fell open. "How did you *know* that? It happened, like, half an hour ago!"

He looked pleased. "I told you, I'm a detective. Anyway, is that what you're thinking about? What went wrong during the challenge?"

She shook her head. "Nothing went wrong. We won."

He arched an eyebrow. "*Nothing* went wrong?"

"No," she said, growing irritated. Clearly sharing a thinking room with Henry had not been a good idea.

"Then why are you here?"

"I'm *thinking*," she returned testily, "about things that happened this morning."

He straightened. "Like what?"

"I don't really want to talk about it."

His eyes slid left, then right. "Was it something suspicious?"

"No, not really."

He lowered his voice to a whisper. "Something . . . like sabotage?"

"Sabotage!" she exclaimed. "Of course not!"

Henry frowned. "Are you sure?"

"Yes, I'm sure. This has to do with Tom Truffleman. And my dad."

"Huh." He tapped his chin. "Are they involved with the sabotage?"

She threw her hands in the air. "What are you even talking about?"

He eyed her carefully. She eyed him back. Then he shrugged and went back to his note-taking.

Alice tried to return to her thoughts, but it was nearly impossible with Henry around, scribbling away. She watched him for a minute, then asked, "Do you always do this? The detective thing, I mean."

He looked up from his notes. "Of course," he said, as if it were perfectly obvious.

"Like, even at school?"

He nodded. "There are mysteries everywhere. But I solved all the ones at my elementary school ages ago. That's why I can't wait to start middle school next year — I'm going to a big school so there should be lots to investigate."

"Huh." Alice had never considered this. "You're not, like . . . scared?"

Henry looked confused. "Of what?"

"Nothing," she said. "Will you go to the same school as Tavi?"

He nodded. "She's a grade ahead of me, so we don't really hang out except when our parents do. I mean, my mom hangs out with her parents. My dad used to before he moved back to Hong Kong —" He stopped himself, then hurried on. "Mr. and Mrs. Sapphire are kind of weird, but nice too. They invited me to come with them when my mom decided she needed some me-time after the divorce." He stopped again and frowned. "Anyway, it's not interesting."

It sounded interesting to Alice, but she knew better than to pry. After a long moment, she asked, "So what about this sabotage?"

"There you are!" James cried, bursting into the library. "I've been looking all over! Richard said he saw you come up here, and — Oh! Hello," he said to Henry. "I'm Alice's dad."

"Oh, I know." Henry raised his pen, ready for note-taking.

James turned back to Alice. "Why did you disappear? We have some serious celebrating to do, you know."

"I just needed a break," she said truthfully. "And you have my room key."

"Oh. I see." He dug in his pocket and handed Alice her key, then glanced at Henry, who was looking him up and down, from his scuffed shoes to his lucky scarf. "Well, Hana has already planned a celebration for the three of us! She booked a table on the terrace for dinner, and afterwards, we're going to a lecture on Victorian astronomy! Isn't that perfect?"

Alice wasn't sure she could take any more astronomy. Or any more Hana.

"She's busy this afternoon, so I thought you and I could take a cooking class. We can learn to make jellied eels!"

Alice's stomach pitched. "I don't think —"

"She can't," Henry piped up.

"I'm sorry?" asked James.

"I can't?" asked Alice.

He shook his head. "We have Bartitsu class."

Alice had completely forgotten about Bartitsu. It sounded nearly as unappealing as making jellied eels. "I don't think —"

"We're sparring partners, remember?"

She did not remember agreeing to this. "What about Tavi?"

"She's learning to commune with the dead." Henry shrugged.

Alice paused to weigh her options. She had no desire to see Hana, but she definitely didn't want to make jellied eels with James.

She wished she'd chosen a different spot to think.

"We should go now!" Henry declared, hopping out of his chair. "We don't want to be late."

"Well, all right," said James, still looking confused. "I'm sure Hana will be delighted to see you."

"She will," Henry agreed.

He ushered Alice out of the library and down the hall. When they were safely out of earshot, he said, "You're welcome."

"Wait, what?" said Alice. "I'm helping *you*. You're the one who needs a sparring partner."

"I saved you from making jellied eels." He grimaced. "*And* from hanging out with your dad."

"I didn't *not* want to hang out with my dad!" she protested.

Henry gave her a knowing look, which she didn't like at all. She was already beginning to regret her decision.

"I might not stay long," she warned as they approached Room 313. "And you can't stop me from leaving."

"Fine, whatever!" He hurried inside, where the class was about to begin.

"Welcome, you two!" Hana greeted them. "I'm so glad you came back!"

Henry skipped into the room, and Alice shuffled after him. "I won't stay long," she told him as they warmed up by swinging their arms in big circles.

"Whatever you say," he replied.

They began by practicing what they'd learned in their previous class, jabbing invisible opponents with canes and umbrellas. Then Hana taught them a new move, which involved swinging their weapon in a big arc that ended in a blow to their opponent's head or shoulder.

After some practice, Hana pulled Leo up to demonstrate how she wanted the class to spar: one student would be the attacker, wielding their weapon as they'd just learned. The other would block them, with both hands gripping their cane or umbrella. She invited them all to pair up and practice.

Henry was on his feet before Hana had finished her instructions. "I'll block first, and you attack, okay?"

"Um, sure." Alice picked up her umbrella. She moved a few feet away, then raised it over her head and swung it down toward him.

"Too easy!" He blocked her swing, then twisted left to knock her off balance. She stumbled but caught herself. "Come on, try again. Harder and faster this time."

"I don't think we're actually supposed to attack each other," she grunted, swinging her umbrella again. Once again Henry blocked it, and this time he slipped out of the way and swung his own umbrella low to the ground, catching Alice's ankle in the hooked handle.

"Did you see that?" he cried. "That was next-level Bartitsu!"

"Let me go," she said crossly, now very much regretting her decision to come.

She was just considering making a run for it when Hana appeared beside them.

"That was impressive, Henry," she said. "I haven't even taught that last move yet."

"I know." He grinned.

She turned to Alice. "I think you need to loosen up a little. Try shrugging your shoulders a bit." She demonstrated, and Henry joined in.

Alice gritted her teeth and shrugged her shoulders.

"Good," said Hana. "Now, when you swing, try to stay loose. It'll hurt less when you make contact."

"Plus, you'll be able to move faster," Henry added.

Alice glared daggers at him.

"I know," said Hana. "Let's spar together, and I'll show you how to block. May I borrow your umbrella, Henry?"

He presented it with a bow. Alice rolled her eyes to the ceiling.

"Great. So now you're going to take a big swing, just like we practiced, and I'll block you. Don't worry," she added, "I've done this a million times. No one is going to get hurt."

Alice took a deep breath and wished she were back in her room — or, better yet, that she and James had never come to Gladstone Manor in the first place. Or, *even better*, that James had never met Hana Holmes, that he'd never decided he needed something more in his life than Alice.

Her chest tightened and her jaw clenched, and she closed her eyes as she swung her umbrella in a big arc, up and over her head and then down toward Hana. They were still closed when she heard Henry yelp and Hana's umbrella clatter to the floor.

She opened her eyes to see Hana keel over, her hands cupped over her face. She gasped, dropping her own umbrella, as the entire class spun to look.

And Henry shrieked, "You killed her! Alice! You killed Hana Holmes!"

CHAPTER

11

Alice knew better than to leave the scene of a crime. She knew that if, for instance, you happened to hit someone with your car, you absolutely had to stay put, otherwise it would be considered a hit-and-run — a very serious crime. This had never actually happened to her, of course, because her father was a very cautious driver, and also, people could hear their old VW Beetle coming from miles away. But still, she knew the rule.

And yet, when Hana crumpled to the floor with her face in her hands, Alice did something she would never have dreamed of doing when she wasn't being accused of murdering her father's girlfriend.

She ran.

She ran out the door and down the hall toward the stairs, then down the stairs to the second floor and down the hall to her room. She unlocked the door and ran over to the bed and dove under the covers, where she found a few cookbooks she'd been reading the previous evening. And she stayed there, hugging *The Victorian Cooking Compendium* and imagining what fate would befall someone who killed her father's new girlfriend and then ran from the scene of the crime.

Of course, Hana couldn't really be dead. That wasn't possible. Was it?

She wasn't sure when she drifted off to sleep, but she awoke with a start when her father burst through the door.

"Alice? Are you there?" He sounded frantic.

"Uh-huh," she mumbled from under the covers.

"Oh, thank god." She heard him cross the room. "I heard about what happened to Hana!"

Alice turned cold, despite all the covers. "Is . . . is she dead?"

"Dead!" he exclaimed. "Of course not! Alice, come out from under there." A second later, he drew back the covers. She blinked until he came into focus, bed-headed and rumpled as usual, but far more distressed.

"She's going to have a black eye," he said, "but probably not a concussion, according to one of the workshop participants who happens to be a paramedic. That was lucky."

Alice wasn't sure if he meant it was lucky to have the paramedic around or lucky that Hana had suffered only a black eye. In any case, she agreed. She was filled with relief and shame and several other things she didn't know how to name — they all burbled inside her, like the medieval goulash her father insisted on making once a week throughout the winter.

He sat down on the bed. "She's going to be fine. I hope. I mean, I'm sure she will."

She watched him wipe his forehead with his scarf, blinking vigorously the way he always did when he was upset. Was he upset because Hana was hurt? Or upset with Alice for hurting her?

Either way, it made her feel prickly all over. Because, yes, she'd hurt Hana, and yes, that was bad. But why did everything have to be about Hana now?

"What about me?" she asked, sitting up suddenly. *The Victorian Cooking Compendium* tumbled to the floor.

James blinked at her. "What about you?"

"You haven't even asked about me and how I'm doing! Well, I'll tell you. I hate this!" she declared. "I hate being at this weird festival, and I hate *Culinary Combat* and Tom Truffleman. And you know what else I hate?" Now she was really getting going. "I hate that you're only upset about Hana. She's all you care about now!"

She knew that wasn't entirely true, but saying it made her feel good.

"Hang on, Alice." James raised a hand. "Is . . . is *that* why you hit her?"

"What?"

"You were angry with Hana and . . ."

"And hit her with an umbrella?" she finished. "You think I hit her on purpose?"

"You didn't?"

"No! I mean, not really. I didn't mean to hit her *that* hard. But I was upset!" she yelled. She wasn't sure she'd ever yelled at her father before. She had yelled *for* him, certainly — like when she was three years old and lost him in a cooking supply store. She'd sat herself down among the cast-iron skillets and hollered at the top of her lungs until he'd appeared.

But this was different. Now she was angry.

She threw the covers off, sending another book flying to the floor.

"Why are there so many cookbooks in here?" he cried. Then he drew a deep breath. "Look, Alice, I know this has been hard on you. I know this is a challenging time. But please don't take it out on Hana."

She froze with her legs halfway out of the bed. He really *did* think that she'd hit Hana on purpose. As though she, Alice Fleck, were some kind of bully, some kind of *thug*! And he really was more concerned about Hana than his own daughter.

"I have to go," she announced. This surprised her, but, like the yelling, it felt right. She had to get out of their room and be by herself. She grabbed her backpack and tossed her phone inside, along with *The Victorian Cooking Compendium*.

He sighed. "Alice, we should talk some more."

"I don't want to." She stuffed her feet into her sneakers and stomped down on the heel, because he hated it when she did that.

And then she did something she'd never done before — never even considered possible.

She walked out and slammed the door so hard the walls shook.

And that also felt right.

Her satisfaction lasted approximately ten seconds, after which she found herself standing in front of the door to Room 224, with her father on the other side. Never having walked out on a fight or slammed a door so hard the walls shook, she had no idea what to do next.

She waited. He'd probably come find her, just as he had found her among the cast-iron skillets that day in the cooking supply store. He'd insist they talk, maybe over pastries or some other treat that would make them both feel better.

She leaned against the door, pressed her cheek to the wood.

She waited some more.

Two men strolled by wearing horseback-riding breeches and top hats. They gave her quizzical looks but thankfully didn't ask questions. Alice tried to look as though she had everything under control and wasn't growing more anxious by the second.

"Are you all right?"

His voice made her jump; he must have been standing on the other side of the door. Had he been waiting there all along?

"Does it hurt very badly?"

"Well, yeah," she replied through the door. "I mean, it's not fair for you to —"

"I just don't know what got into her. Honestly, she's never been an aggressive child."

Alice's mouth fell open. He wasn't talking to her. He was talking to Hana! He'd phoned *Hana* instead of coming to look for her.

She stumbled back from the door, then hurried away down the hall.

She was going to cry — that was a given, it was just a matter of time. And when it happened, she needed to be someplace where she wouldn't have to talk to anyone.

She left the east wing and headed into the west, past a grandfather clock chiming three o'clock, past a room full of people practicing calligraphy. She kept going until she came to a quiet corner with a window looking out onto the terrace.

She sat down on the floor and pulled out her phone, hoping to find an apology text from her father, since apparently he knew how to text now. But she had no new messages. She tossed the phone back in her backpack.

"Alice!"

She looked up to see a girl in a long, white lace dress walking toward her. It took her a moment to recognize Tavi's red-velvet hair, pinned in a knot atop her head.

"Oh, it's you!"

"Cool dress, right?" Tavi grinned. "I found it in the costume room. It was perfect for the workshop I just went to — we learned to talk to the dead! Have you been waiting for me?"

"Um, no," said Alice. "Why?"

"This is my room." Tavi pointed to the nearest door. "Our room, I mean. Are you coming in?"

Was she? Alice wasn't sure. She didn't want to be in Tavi's room when she inevitably started to cry, but neither did she want to be sitting by herself in the hallway. She nodded, picked herself up and followed Tavi inside.

The room was small and cozy, furnished with a soft pink couch with a backrest on one end and two twin beds. One bed had clearly been slept in; the other was piled high with clothes.

"Sorry," Tavi said. "I wasn't sure you'd come, so I took over your bed. But try out that couch — it's an *actual* fainting couch, and it's super comfy."

"Okay." Alice perched on the fainting couch.

Tavi sat on the slept-in bed and looked at her expectantly. "So, what do you think?"

Alice opened her mouth to say that it was a very nice room, but what came out instead, to her horror, was a big, gasping sob.

"Oh!" Tavi bolted for the bathroom and returned with a box of tissues. She put the box in Alice's lap and sat back down to face her. "What's wrong?" When Alice could only sob, Tavi added, "It's okay. Sometimes you just have to cry it out first."

She was so much kinder and less intimidating than Alice

would ever have guessed, and it made her cry harder. When the tears finally subsided, she blew her nose and wiped her eyes. "Sorry," she murmured.

"Don't be." Tavi shrugged. "Now, do you want to tell me what's wrong? Or I could guess, if you'd rather. I'm pretty good at figuring out what's wrong with people. My dad's a psychologist, you know."

Alice didn't think this was a good idea. "I just had a fight with my dad. I've never done that before."

"Never?" Tavi looked shocked. "Like, never *ever*?"

Alice shook her head.

"Wow. You guys must get along really well. I get along with my parents too, but we still fight. Especially at Christmas. Last year we actually canceled it completely and celebrated in February. My mom finds it too stressful." She drew her legs up onto the bed. "The point is, Alice, fights happen. It's going to be okay."

Alice nodded, but she wasn't so sure.

"Do you want to tell me what happened?"

Alice recalled how good it had felt to tell Tavi all about the drama of the first cooking challenge. Maybe it was because she was the daughter of a psychologist? Or maybe this was how it felt to talk freely to a good friend.

She wavered for only a moment before letting it all spill out. She told Tavi about how she'd closed her eyes and swung her umbrella at Hana, maybe a bit harder than she'd meant to. And how she'd opened her eyes to find Hana on the floor and Henry accusing her of murder. She even admitted to running from the scene of the crime.

Tavi stayed quiet while Alice talked, nodding every now and then or making thoughtful humming noises. "Wow. Okay," she said once Alice had stopped to catch her breath. "Do you want to know what I think?"

Alice nodded.

"First off, Hana's going to be fine. You said it was just a black eye in the end, right? She'll probably have an ugly bruise, but those things heal. My mom got a black eye last summer at the medieval reenactment festival. She got hit by the hilt of another knight's sword. Dad and I warned her she wasn't ready for a duel, but she wouldn't listen. It looked kind of gross, but it went away in a few weeks."

"Oh. Okay." This made Alice feel a tiny bit better.

"But now let's talk about Hana." Tavi tented her fingers below her chin. "Clearly you don't like her."

"Well, I don't *hate* her," said Alice. "I just think we were better off without her. At least, I was. I think my dad was too."

"And you don't want her as a mom," Tavi observed. "Wait, do you have a mom?"

"Oh. Um. No," said Alice. "I mean, technically, yes. But also . . . no." It was hard to explain, which was why she tried to avoid it.

Tavi waited.

Alice sighed. "Okay," she said. And she told Tavi about Lavinia Lomond. Her mother. Technically.

James and Lavinia had met in France when they were both university students. Lavinia was an archaeologist, passionate about ancient cave art. James was a budding culinary historian, passionate about cave-aged cheese. They met in the Pyrenees mountains on the same day James found his lucky green scarf on a train.

They fell in love almost immediately — according to James, it happened over a picnic in a mountain meadow, where they shared a crispy baguette, a dry red wine, some nice Camembert. He was smitten with Lavinia Lomond.

And Lavinia was smitten with cave art. It was her calling, she explained: she believed she was born to decipher the markings left behind by some of the very first Homo sapiens to walk the earth. And when she found out she was pregnant, she knew right away she couldn't be a mother. You can't raise a child in a cave, she reasoned, and James agreed it wouldn't be ideal. But he wanted to be a father. So when baby Alice was born, James brought her back to Canada to raise her alone.

To her credit, Lavinia maintained a consistent (if somewhat unenthusiastic) interest in Alice for quite some time. Once a year she'd visit, and the three of them would go for lunch — usually someplace French, "for old times' sake," as James would say. But Lavinia didn't seem to care what or where they ate — she'd gulp down her ratatouille as if she couldn't wait to escape. She wouldn't even take off her giant sunglasses, as her eyes were unaccustomed to the light outside her cave.

It wasn't the hasty lunches that Alice disliked, or even the strange questions Lavinia asked her, like what kind of tools she'd learned to use, and whether she was aware that cave-dwelling Neanderthals had also had ginger-colored hair (James later insisted Lavinia hadn't meant this as an insult, but simply as an interesting connection).

What Alice disliked most was how, after they'd said goodbye to Lavinia for another year, James seemed to disappear inside himself, quiet and sad and far away. She tried her best to distract him; she even made up a rule that after their lunch with Lavinia they had to do something fun. One year it was go-karting; the next year, a trampoline gym. Inevitably, though, they'd return to their apartment and James would go sit quietly by himself, sometimes for hours on end.

Even at five years old, Alice could tell that he still loved Lavinia. And Lavinia didn't feel the same way about him.

When Alice was ten, Lavinia stopped visiting altogether. Her research had really picked up, she explained in a letter smeared with cave dust. She was on the brink of a momentous discovery — they'd read about it soon in *National Geographic*. She barely had time to eat, let alone fly halfway across the world for lunch.

Alice was perfectly fine with that.

"Hmm." Tavi stroked her chin, considering the story. "After all that, you'd think he might not want to be in a relationship again."

"Right?" Alice agreed. "Exactly."

"But the heart wants what the heart wants, I guess. That's what my dad says. He knew right away that my mom was the person for him, before they'd even said hello. They met at a Charles Dickens reenactment day," she added, "over a big pot of gruel."

"Huh." Alice wasn't sure what to do with this piece of information.

"Okay." Tavi clapped her hands. "You know what you need, Alice? You need some time to yourself. Some me-time."

"Me-time?" Alice thought of Henry's mother at her yoga retreat. She wasn't sure she needed that.

"Or at least some time away from your dad and Hana. So, here's what we'll do." Tavi hopped off her bed. "First, we'll have a sleepover! You'll stay here with me tonight — I'll clear the clothes off your bed. It'll be fun!"

A sleepover. Alice gulped. "Oh. Um . . ."

"Super fun," Tavi assured her. "But we'll have to tell your dad about the plan. That's the thing with parents: they worry way less if you just tell them where you are and what you're doing."

"Okay," Alice said uncertainly.

"You don't have to talk to him, though," Tavi went on. "You can text! That's what I do when I fight with my parents. It's so much easier."

They sat side by side on the fainting couch and composed a text, telling James that Alice was staying with Tavi and that he didn't have to worry about her. As Alice hit send, she couldn't help but hope he would protest, knowing how she felt about sleepovers.

He texted back immediately: As you wish, sous-chef. But do you want to talk first?

"Do you?" asked Tavi.

No thanks, Alice told him.

Let's talk tomorrow then, he said. Have fun and let me know if you need anything.

"Great!" said Tavi.

Alice forced her mouth into a smile so she wouldn't start crying again. "Just great," she agreed.

"So now we need to do something to take your mind off everything. Something really different." Tavi stood and smoothed her dress. "And I know just the thing."

"What's that?" Alice asked, hoping it would involve watching a show on Tavi's tablet. She'd even watch the one about deadly desserts, though it sounded really creepy.

Tavi put her hands on her hips. "We're going to go hunt down some ghosts."

CHAPTER

12

"You know ghosts don't exist, right?" Henry said flatly.

"That's what I said," Alice agreed, relieved for once to have Henry around and hopeful he might talk some sense into Tavi. Truth be told, Alice wasn't sure whether ghosts existed or not, and she didn't particularly want to find out.

"That's where you're both wrong," said Tavi. "Cultures around the world have believed in ghosts, like, forever. Even now, almost half of North Americans believe in them — I learned that in my workshop today." She leaned back on the stone steps of the terrace, where they'd settled after dinner to watch some guests practice dance steps on the lawn. "I'm surprised you don't know this, Henry." She poked him in the ribs.

He sniffed. "I don't keep that kind of information in my brain attic."

"I'm sorry, what?" Tavi laughed. "Your *brain attic*?"

He nodded. "Sherlock Holmes said the brain is like an attic, and you have to stock it with the right furniture. You can't fit everything in there, so you have to choose carefully. Obviously, he was talking about information. If you're a detective, it's especially important to be selective about what you keep. And ghosts," he concluded, "have no place in my brain attic."

"That's okay, they can live in my brain attic," Tavi said happily. "Oh my gosh, do you think there's an attic in the manor? Attics are prime real estate for ghosts!"

Henry rolled his eyes to the darkening sky. Then he turned to Alice. "How's Hana doing?"

Any feelings of goodwill she'd had for him dissolved on the spot, like gelatin in water. "She's fine," she said coldly. "I think. Anyway, she's not *dead*."

He nodded. "I knew she wasn't."

"But let's get back to the ghosts," Tavi cut in. "The Victorians liked to consult the spirits about all kinds of things, everything from who they should marry to what they should serve for dinner."

Henry snorted.

She ignored him. "They'd hire these people called mediums, who could talk to the ghosts and report back, kind of like interpreters. Sometimes, though, the mediums were just pretending to talk to ghosts. I guess some of them were only in it for the money."

"Because *ghosts don't exist*," said Henry.

"But *sometimes*, the mediums were the real deal," Tavi insisted. "Anyway, my point is that there's no better place to look for Victorian ghosts than a Victorian festival at a Victorian manor. And what's the harm in looking?"

The harm, Alice thought, was that they might actually find one. She was worried enough about her impending sleepover — if they actually encountered a ghost, she might never sleep again.

But she didn't say any of this aloud, and Henry stayed quiet too.

"Great, then it's settled! We'll head out as soon as it's dark."

The sun was dipping behind the dancers, casting long shadows on the lawn. Tavi's parents were among them, clearly more skilled than most of the others. Sven and Samir were out there as well, clearly more skilled at cooking than dancing. They waved merrily at Alice, and she waved back.

James, however, was nowhere to be seen. Part of her longed to find him and apologize, to make everything feel normal again. But she also wanted *him* to find *her* and apologize, because didn't she deserve that?

Thinking about it made her head hurt.

"Okay, fine, I'll come with you," Henry said. "But only because it's a good opportunity to do some investigating. *Not* because I believe in ghosts."

"Fine by me." Tavi reached out for a fist bump. Henry eyed her fist for a long moment before tapping it carefully with his own. "What are you investigating?"

"I'm working on a case." He patted the notebook in his lap. "That's all I can say for now."

Alice shrugged, not wanting to give him the satisfaction of knowing she was curious.

Soon the sun disappeared, and the dancers began to drift indoors.

"We should go change our clothes," Tavi said. "Ooh, we should find costumes!"

"No costumes," Henry said flatly. "They would attract too much attention, and we need to go unnoticed. We should wear dark clothes."

"Ghostly clothes," Tavi added in a whisper, and she laughed when he rolled his eyes again.

Alice hadn't thought to pack clothes before she stormed out

of her father's room, so Tavi offered to lend her some. They ran upstairs to her room, where she dug through the pile of clothes on Alice's bed and pulled out a black hoodie. It hung down to Alice's knees, but it was soft and cozy. She zipped it up to her chin and felt immediately better — until the phone in her pocket buzzed.

Everything all right, sous-chef?

The sight of his message filled her with relief, anger and sadness all at once. She responded with a thumbs-up emoji.

Be sure to get enough sleep tonight! We have to defend our title bright and early tomorrow.

"Defend our . . . Oh!" She'd completely forgotten about the next cooking challenge.

"Alice?" Tavi was standing in the doorway, wearing black jeans and a black turtleneck. "Ready to go?"

She looked from her friend to her father's message and back, weighing her options. She could spend the evening preparing for another torturous session with Tom Truffleman. Or she could search Gladstone Manor for ghosts.

The decision was surprisingly easy. "Ready," she said, pocketing her phone.

They found Henry waiting in the library, wearing a brown plaid hat with flaps that folded up and fastened on top of his head.

"You said no costumes!" Tavi cried.

"It's not a costume," he replied defensively. "It's called a deerstalker. Sherlock Holmes wore one."

"I *know*." Tavi crossed her arms over her chest. "And that makes it one hundred percent a costume."

"It's really more of a uniform," he sniffed.

"Great, so where are we going?" Alice asked before a fight could erupt. She'd had enough fighting for one day.

"Well, it's games night in the parlor, so we want to avoid that," said Henry. "Too many people."

Tavi nodded, still looking put out. "I thought we could start in the ballroom — Richard set up some kind of exhibit there. I can't remember the name, but —"

"It's called 'Victorian Inventions and Oddities,'" said Henry.

"Sounds good," Alice said. "Let's go."

But when they reached the ballroom, they found a sign on the door that told them the exhibit had closed at six o'clock. It was now almost nine.

"Too bad," said Alice. "What should we do now?"

"This." Henry pulled on the door handle. The door swung wide open.

"Wait, but it's closed!" Alice protested. "The sign says so."

"The door's not locked," he pointed out. "An unlocked door is basically an invitation to walk in." He stepped inside. "Coming?"

"I guess he has a point." Tavi followed.

Alice wasn't convinced, but she didn't want to get left behind. She slipped in after them and closed the door behind her.

Moonlight streamed through the windows, illuminating the ballroom with silvery-blue light. Though she'd been there before, for the welcome ceremony, she'd been more focused on the guests than the room itself. Now she noted that the walls were painted forest-green and decorated with enormous paintings like those in the Great Hall.

The exhibit stood on the far side of the room, next to a painting of some racehorses charging down a track. They tiptoed over, casting moonlit shadows on the wood floors, and Alice couldn't help but wonder if the ghosts of Gladstone Manor might be watching them. She tried not to think about it.

"Look! Taxidermy!" Tavi pointed at a table full of dead animals arranged in lifelike poses. Alice could make out a squirrel, a fox and what looked like a wild boar.

"That's creepy," she said. Henry agreed.

"The Victorians loved taxidermy," said Tavi. "Especially the weird stuff." She told them about a taxidermist who'd made dioramas with animals in human settings, like squirrels at a garden party and kittens in a schoolhouse.

Alice made a mental note to tell Mat about the creepy Victorian dioramas — and make him swear he'd never use dead animals in his own art.

They moved on to peruse some Victorian inventions: an old rotary-dial telephone, some postage stamps, a typewriter, an electric flashbulb and even a flush toilet. There were strange inventions too, like a hooked cane that turned into an umbrella, a butterfly net *and* a flute.

"That would be great for Bartitsu," said Henry.

Alice turned away. She didn't want to think about Bartitsu. Then Tavi gasped. "Look!"

Alice turned back to find her standing beside what looked like a very old scooter, with a large box on the foot deck and cables connecting the handle grip to the front wheel.

"Is that actually motorized?" asked Henry.

"Looks like it." Tavi consulted the sign beside the scooter. "It's called an Autoped, and it was invented just after the Victorian age. Apparently a suffragette named Lady Norman used to ride one just like this around London. That's so cool!"

Alice nodded, wondering if Hana knew about Lady Norman, the scooting suffragette. Then she winced, recalling what she'd done to Hana.

Tavi turned to face them, eyes gleaming in the moonlight. "Should we try it?"

"Yes!" said Henry. "I mean, no." He glanced at the door.

"*Definitely* not," Alice agreed. Riding an antique scooter was absolutely against the rules.

"But what if we took really good care of it? No one would know."

Henry chewed his lip. "It might not even work," he pointed out. But when Tavi flipped a switch on the frame, the motor hummed to life.

"We really shouldn't," Alice insisted, but even she had to admit it was tempting. She hadn't ridden a scooter since she'd outgrown the one James bought at a garage sale when she was five. And she'd never ridden one with a motor.

They agreed that Tavi would steer, since it was her idea. Henry stood behind her, and Alice came third, clutching Henry's shoulders as they zipped around the room. Lady Norman's scooter was surprisingly peppy considering it was over a hundred years old.

"This is so fun!" Tavi squealed.

"Turn right!" Henry's deerstalker flew off his head and bounced across the floor. "You're going to hit the wall!"

Tavi swerved suddenly and the scooter tipped sideways, but she righted it just in time. Alice gasped, then laughed. She couldn't believe she was riding an antique scooter around an off-limits exhibit — and what's more, that it felt so deliciously good. Tavi was right: she *had* needed a distraction. And this was —

Suddenly, Tavi hit the brakes and they lurched to a halt

beside the taxidermy table. Henry and Alice pitched forward, then tumbled onto the floor.

"Ow! What happened?" Alice cried.

Tavi held up a hand for silence. "Did you hear that?"

"Hear what?" Henry rubbed the knee he'd landed on. "That hurt!"

She shushed him just as the door clicked, then creaked open. A long beam of light fell onto the floor.

"Under the table!" Tavi commanded. They ducked under the tablecloth, and Tavi yanked the scooter in beside them.

After a long pause, a man called, "Is someone there?"

Henry lifted the tablecloth so they could peer out. "It's Richard," he whispered. "He's coming in."

Alice's heart began to hammer. What had they been thinking, riding an antique scooter around an off-limits exhibit? *Of course* they were going to get caught!

"Just stay quiet, and breathe," Tavi murmured. Alice took the deepest, quietest breath she could. Beside her, Henry did the same.

Something skittered across the floor. A moment later, they heard a high-pitched whine.

"It's the dog!" Henry whispered.

"See, Roslyn? There's no one here," Richard said from the doorway. The whippet began to pace around the room, close to the walls. She paused under a painting of a silver racehorse and whined again.

"Do you think she smells us?" Alice hissed. Tavi and Henry shushed her.

"What's gotten into you?" asked Richard. "Do you need another walk? Or do you smell a ghost?"

Tavi gasped. Alice and Henry shushed her.

After a long pause, Roslyn trotted back to the door. Moments later, it clicked shut again.

They let out their breath all at once.

"That was so close!" Henry collapsed on the floor.

"I can't believe she didn't find us!" said Tavi. "Can you imagine what would have happened if she had?"

Alice didn't want to imagine. She lay down on the cool floor beside Henry, taking deep breaths to slow her hammering heart.

"Do you think the ghosts take the scooter out for a ride at night?" Tavi asked.

Henry snorted. "Maybe if they actually existed."

"You heard Richard! There *must* be ghosts around here. He's probably seen them, gliding from room to room in the dead of night, stirring up all kinds of trouble." She shivered happily.

Henry shook his head. "Someone might be stirring up trouble in the dead of night, but it's not a ghost."

"What do you mean?" asked Alice.

"It's a theory I'm working on," he replied.

"You keep saying that." Tavi elbowed him. "What is it? Tell us more, Detective Oh."

Henry gave them a long, serious look. "Sabotage."

"What?" Tavi exclaimed. "You mean the ghost?"

"There's no ghost," he told her. "But there might be a saboteur — that's someone who sabotages."

"Sabotages what?" asked Alice.

He paused dramatically. "*Culinary Combat.*"

"*What?*"

"Don't you see what's going on?" Henry held up a finger.

122

"First, an oven gets turned off in the middle of a challenge."

"Except it didn't," she told him. "François forgot to turn it on."

"But he insisted he *did*," said Henry.

"There's no way someone could have turned off his oven in the middle of a challenge," she argued. "Not with all those cameras around. Trust me. I was *there*."

"But remember what happened to Diana this morning?"

Alice tried to recall — it felt like years ago. "You mean how she mixed up the sugar and salt?" Henry nodded. "They weren't labeled, that's all. Nothing got sabotaged. Also, how did you find out . . ." She stopped and shook her head. "Never mind." Clearly, Henry *was* a first-class snoop.

"Were the jars labeled the first day of the competition?" he asked.

She tried to recall but couldn't.

"Maybe it was a poltergeist!" Tavi suggested. Henry gave her a tired look.

Suddenly, Alice wanted very badly to turn on a light — or better yet, all the lights. She was done with sitting in the dark, under a table of taxidermy, discussing how a saboteur might be making the cooking competition even more impossible than it already was.

"I think we should go," she said.

"Yes." Tavi crawled out from under the table and hopped to her feet. "After one more spin on the scooter!"

Alice declined, no longer in the mood for scooting around the ballroom. Tavi and Henry sped off, and she sat and watched them, wondering what the next day had in store for her, and whether Henry's theory could possibly be right.

Her phone buzzed and she pulled it out to find a good-night text from James: two sleepy-face emojis and a full moon. She was fairly certain he'd never used emojis before.

She tried to come up with a message to send back, but eventually she just gave up and let it go unanswered. For all he knew, she was already fast asleep in Tavi's room.

CHAPTER
13

Alice awoke the next morning cocooned in a big, cozy hoodie. She was in Tavi's room, still wearing Tavi's clothes. Which could only mean one thing.

She had survived a sleepover.

Not only that, she'd fallen asleep immediately after they'd returned from the ballroom and hadn't even woken during the night, let alone had to sneak back to her father's room and sleep in her own bed. It was cause for celebration!

Or it would have been had her phone not buzzed with a text.

I don't see you in the dining room — have you eaten already? We have to be at the Great Hall at 8!

She blinked at the message from her father, then remembered the competition. The clock on her phone read 7:45.

She bolted out of bed and wriggled out of Tavi's hoodie. Underneath, she was wearing the same clothes she'd worn the day before, and there appeared to be a stain on her T-shirt. Hopefully her apron would cover it.

She folded the hoodie and left it on her pillow. In the bed beside hers, Tavi was still asleep, her hair a red-velvet nest on her pillow, her mouth wide open. As quickly as possible, Alice braided her hair, grabbed her backpack and slipped out the door.

She jogged down the stairs and across the lobby just as Richard came through the front door with Roslyn, who was dressed in a red coat with a fur-lined hood. The whippet yapped as Alice ran past, and Alice avoided eye contact.

When she reached the Great Hall, she found all the contestants standing outside the door. According to her phone, it was 8:05. They ought to be inside, preparing for the challenge.

"Alice!" James popped out of the huddle, looking as though he too had slept in his clothes. He started toward her, arms wide, and the sight made her weak with relief. Maybe they could pretend yesterday hadn't happened. Maybe everything could just go back to normal.

Suddenly he stopped, and his arms fell to his sides. "Um, how are you?" he asked. "Everything all right?"

So much for normal. "I'm fine," she said stiffly. "I just slept in."

"Right." He nodded. After an awkward pause, he asked, "Did you have breakfast?"

She shook her head.

"Alice —"

"I'm fine," she insisted, though now that he'd mentioned it, she actually was hungry. "What's going on? Why are we out here?"

"We're not sure," said Tina. "They won't let us in."

"They're probably deciding what kind of torture to inflict on us today," Toni added.

"We missed you last night, Alice." Tina smiled at her. "We all went stargazing under the full moon!"

"It was very romantic." Samir smiled at Sven.

Had Hana gone with them? Alice decided that she didn't want to know.

"What did you get up to?" asked Tina.

She paused, recalling everything she, Tavi and Henry had done the previous night. "I went to bed early," she lied.

"They should have let us in by now," Phyllis grumbled at the door. "All this secrecy is unnerving."

Everyone agreed. Alice rubbed her goosebumped arms, wishing she'd kept Tavi's hoodie. Beside her, James was quietly shifting from one foot to the other, and she wished he would stop being so awkward. It was making her feel even more awkward, and pretty soon they would be on camera, acting awkward together.

She wished she didn't have to cook.

Finally, the door opened, and Jasmina peered out. "Sorry to keep you guys waiting," she said. "Please, come in." Alice noted dark circles under the producer's eyes. She had a feeling they weren't from stargazing under the full moon.

They filed into the Great Hall and looked around. There were four workstations left, and each one had returned to its original size.

"See? Everything's back to normal." Tina nudged Toni. "Nothing to worry about."

Jasmina cleared her throat. "Okay everyone, gather around, please. I've got some news."

Toni shot her sister an I-told-you-so look.

"There's been a . . . a change in plans."

"Not again!" groaned Samir.

"I knew it," Toni grumped. "How are you torturing us today?"

"We're not torturing . . ." Jasmina began, then stopped herself. "Okay. Today, Tom wants to see the lead competitors — that's

Phyllis, Tina, James and Sven — cook by themselves, without their assistants."

"What?" cried Sven and Samir.

"No way!" exclaimed the twins.

"Surely you're joking," said James, but Jasmina shook her head. He turned to Alice. "I'm so sorry, sous-chef."

Alice nodded, stunned by the news. She was sorry too.

And she was also relieved — *immensely* relieved. This meant no cameras capturing her every move, no microphones recording her every word and no Tom Truffleman criticizing her every mistake. Outwardly, she tried to look disappointed. Inwardly, she cheered.

"Tom came up with this idea last night, and he refused to change his mind," Jasmina went on. "Believe me, I tried. But it's just for today. The assistants will be allowed to cook in the next challenge."

She led Alice, Samir and Toni off set, where three chairs awaited them. There, she said, they could watch the challenge as long as they stayed quiet and didn't try to help.

"This isn't fair," Samir moaned as he sank into his chair.

"Truffleman is the worst," Toni grunted.

Miranda Summers arrived as the competitors were settling into their workstations; judging by the look on her face as she took in the scene, the change was news to her as well.

Moments before filming began, Tom Truffleman swept through the doors. He looked from the competitors standing solo at their stations to the assistants slumped in their chairs. A smile spread across his face.

Toni and Samir muttered curse words under their breath.

"Today's challenge will be a tricky one," Miranda announced once the cameras were rolling. "The contestants will have three hours to make . . ." She paused. "A deep-dish . . . *pigeon* pie!" She made a face. "Sounds gross, right? I thought so too. But apparently the Victorians were into it."

Alice nodded. She'd never cooked a pigeon pie herself, but she'd seen it in cookbooks, and if she remembered correctly it wasn't that different from cooking any other meat pie. Which meant her father, who'd once made *fifty-seven* pork pies, could practically do it in his sleep.

She saw him straighten and smile. And though she was still angry with him, she was relieved to know he'd be fine.

"But wait, there's more!" Miranda went on. "Your recipe won't tell you how to make the crust — you'll have to figure that out yourself, along with the oven temperature and baking times. Your pie must be perfectly cooked, and it also has to look beautiful — Tom wants to see a fancy lattice top made with braided pie dough."

"A lattice top with —" Alice breathed. "Oh no." She watched the smile fade from her father's face.

"What's wrong?" Toni whispered.

She gulped. "He can't braid."

"What? Like, not at all?"

She shook her head. Her father was very good at many things, but when it came to braiding, he was absolutely, completely hopeless. She'd tried countless times to teach him — with her hair, with ribbons, with strands of dough — but he simply couldn't do it. If a recipe involved braiding, Alice always did it herself.

"Uh-oh," said Toni.

"Anything to add, Tom?" Miranda asked.

The judge nodded. "You might be thinking that pigeons are nothing more than rats that can fly. And you're not wrong." He grimaced. "But they are worth eating when they're young and tender. That's the kind of meat you'll be cooking, and I expect it to be delicious."

Miranda looked ill. "If you say so. Okay, everyone, get cooking!"

With that, the third challenge began. The competitors scattered, gathering meat, flour, eggs, butter and spices from the fridges and the shelves. The crew moved with them, angling lights, adjusting sound levels and cleaning up spills. It was fascinating to watch from off set, and strange to think that when the show aired viewers would miss so much of the action: they would only ever see the competitors, host and judge.

Everyone began by preparing their pie fillings, mixing the meat with spices like nutmeg and sage. Soon the hall was filled with mouth-watering smells, and Alice's stomach began to rumble. She wished she hadn't skipped breakfast.

"Fun fact about Tom Truffleman," Samir whispered. "He really can't stand pigeons. Years ago, I saw a video of him freaking out when one crossed his path — like, actually screaming. The video went viral around the time he launched *Bare-knuckled Bakers*. Apparently he was attacked by a flock of pigeons as a kid and never really got over it."

Toni laughed. "That must be why he likes pigeon pie."

Alice shuddered. "That's awful."

James had just begun to work on his pastry when Miranda sidled up to his workstation and propped her elbows on the countertop. "What happened to your lucky scarf, James?" she asked.

He frowned. "Oh, I couldn't find it this morning. I looked everywhere, but no luck. To be honest, I feel lost without it."

Alice hadn't even noticed he wasn't wearing his scarf! And she could see the worry-wrinkle between his eyebrows, which meant he was upset.

It wasn't lucky anyway, she tried to tell him telepathically. *Don't think about it. Just cook.*

She watched closely as he prepared his pie crust, her hands kneading imaginary dough along with him, then rolling it out and lining the pan. He filled the pie with the meat he'd prepared and smoothed out the top. And then it was time for the final step: creating a fancy braided lattice top.

"I hate making lattice-topped pies — they're so finicky," whispered Toni. "Good thing Tina's doing it and not me."

Alice nodded. Lattice-topped pies *were* finicky. First, you had to cut your dough into long, even strips. Then you had to lay them on top of the pie, half parallel and half perpendicular, and weave some strips under and some strips over each other, eventually creating a neat, crisscross pattern. And you had to do it quickly, while your dough was still cold. Otherwise it was impossible to work with.

And that was just a normal lattice. James had the added challenge of braiding the strands before weaving them.

She watched him cut three long strands of dough and lay them on the countertop. He crossed one strand over the next, then frowned and uncrossed it.

Take the outside strand and put it in the middle, she urged him silently. *Come on, we've been through this!*

He tried again, stopped again, bit his lip and tried once more. The wrinkle between his eyebrows deepened.

Alice's fingers twitched. Now the other competitors were putting the finishing touches on their pies — she could see Tina decorating hers with little heart-shaped pieces of dough. "Come on," she whispered, envisioning all the things she could do with the dough. She'd seen a pie on PHOMO covered with little pastry flowers and vines that appeared to be climbing a trellis. She would do that. Or, she would make a flock of little pastry pigeons and assemble them around the edge — except that might upset Tom Truffleman, if he hated pigeons as much as Samir said.

"Darn it!" James grunted as one of the strands fell apart in his hands. Two cameras immediately descended on his station. He glanced over at Alice and shrugged apologetically.

Suddenly, she was seized by a desire — practically a *need* — to dash onto the set, grab the dough from his hands and braid it herself. She squirmed in her chair, and Toni put an arm around her shoulders, whispering that everything would be okay.

But Alice could see Tom Truffleman standing by the fridges, watching her father's disastrous attempts to braid dough. The look on his face told her that Toni was wrong: it would not be okay.

Eventually, James gave up. He placed some straggly pieces of dough on top of the pie filling, criss-crossing them in random places, then slid his creation into the oven and shut the door. "I'm sorry," he mouthed to Alice.

She felt as if she'd been stabbed with an umbrella. She put her head in her hands.

While the pies were baking, the cleaning crew wiped down the workstations and rearranged equipment. There was nothing for the contestants to do but wait for their pies to bake and talk to Miranda as she strolled around the room.

Her first stop was James's workstation. "So, tell me about this scarf of yours," she said. "What makes it lucky?"

"Oh, come *on*," said Alice. As if the challenge hadn't been painful enough!

James's face brightened as he told Miranda about finding

the scarf on a train in the Pyrenees. It was, he explained, the day he'd met Alice's mother.

Miranda's eyes widened. "James, that's so sweet! Oh my gosh, and you're *single*?"

"Um, no," he said. "I'm in a relationship, remember?"

"Oh, right." She looked disappointed. "I was hoping to set you up with someone. Maybe find a mother for sweet little Allie?"

Alice groaned. Could it get any worse?

"Matchmaking is my favorite thing to do, you know," Miranda went on. "I think it might be my true calling. Did you know my first job was an internship on the hit reality TV show *Match Made in Hollywood*?"

"Was it now?" James said politely.

Thankfully, the videographer decided she'd heard enough and wandered off, sparing James the details and Alice from dying of embarrassment. They went back to waiting for his pie to cook.

Finally, with only five minutes left on the clock, the contestants pulled their pies out of their ovens. Alice could see that Sven's was beautiful; she'd never seen a lattice so perfect and precise. Tina's looked amazing too, adorned with dozens of tiny pastry hearts.

Alice was just wondering how Phyllis had fared when a shriek pierced the air, followed by a resounding crash. Pie crust and cooked pigeon meat went flying; Miranda screamed and ducked for cover.

"My pie!" cried Phyllis.

"Oh my gosh!" Toni jumped out of her chair. "Did she just —"

"Drop her pie!" Samir finished. "The whole thing!"

The entire camera crew ran to film the disaster: a deep-dish pigeon pie, splattered on the floor, on the walls, on Phyllis's tweed slacks. Phyllis herself was standing stock-still, her hands in oven mitts pressed to her forehead.

"Phyllis!" James hurried toward her, only to slip on the splattered pie and slide across the floor, arms flailing.

"Nobody else move!" Jasmina commanded as the cleanup crew thundered on set with mops and rags. "Phyllis, are you all right?"

She nodded, dazed. "I . . . I don't know what happened."

"Oh, poor Phyllis," Toni moaned.

"Why did she drop it?" Samir wondered.

"I don't know," said Toni, "but I'm afraid that's it for her."

"Wait, really?" Alice looked at her. "They'd send her home for dropping her pie? But that's so unfair!"

"Well, Truffleman isn't exactly forgiving. Someone else would really have to mess up in order for Phyllis to stay."

Alice couldn't get a good look at her father's pie, but she could tell from his face as he returned to his workstation that it wasn't pretty.

As soon as the judging began, Tom Truffleman confirmed her suspicions. "It's nicely baked, with decent flavor," he said, after taking a tiny bite. "But that is *not* a lattice top." He poked at James's pie. "And *that* is definitely not a braid. This is an abomination, James. Don't you know how to braid?"

Red-faced, James mumbled that he always relied on Alice to braid.

"You can't rely on a *twelve-year-old girl*!" the judge cried, as if James had just told him he relied on Alice to drive their car. "This is a real disappointment, you know. Especially considering how well you did in the last challenge."

Alice gripped the arms of her chair. Tom Truffleman *was* the worst.

Also, why *couldn't* you rely on a twelve-year-old girl?

James mumbled an apology, and the judge moved on. He deemed both Tina's and Sven's pies edible and attractive.

"Now that's what a braid should look like!" He tossed James a pointed look.

Alice envisioned overturning a pie on the judge's head.

Last came Phyllis, who had nothing to show for all the hours she'd spent cooking. "I just don't know what happened," she said, still looking dazed. "My oven mitts are covered in oil, and the pie just slipped through them. But . . . but I don't know how they got that way! I can't remember spilling any oil."

"Well, there's nothing I can do about it," Truffleman sniffed. "You have nothing for me to judge."

Phyllis's shoulders sagged. "I know."

"That's awful," groaned Samir.

"Such bad luck," sighed Toni.

And Alice would have agreed had Henry's voice not popped into her head: *Don't you see what's going on?*

It *could* have been an accident, she reasoned. But even she was having a hard time believing that.

And what if it wasn't an accident? The competition was grueling enough to begin with — watching it from off set had given her a new appreciation of that. If a saboteur was at work, making things even worse for the competitors, well, that was unfathomably unfair.

While Miranda announced that Sven had won the pigeon pie challenge, Alice pulled her phone out of her backpack and sent Tavi a text.

Meet me in the library? I need to talk.

Tavi texted back: Be there in 10.

Great, Alice replied. And bring Henry too.

CHAPTER
14

By the time Alice reached the library, Tavi and Henry were already there, waiting in the leather armchairs. She headed for the third chair and collapsed into it, breathless; she'd come straight from the Great Hall after filming had ended. She hadn't even waited to talk to her father — partly because he'd looked ready to dash after Phyllis, who'd left the hall immediately, and partly because she didn't know what to say.

"Thanks for coming, guys," she began.

"Wait!" Tavi hopped up. "This feels like a door-closer."

"A what?"

"A door-closer. That's what my parents say when they have to talk about something and don't want me to hear. Should I close the door?"

"Oh. Yes, please."

Tavi shut the door, then turned the lock. "Because an unlocked door is basically an invitation to walk in," she said, quoting Henry. Then she jumped back into her chair and motioned for Alice to proceed. Henry opened his notebook and uncapped his pen.

Alice recounted the morning's events, wincing through the part about the pie dough.

"Yikes. And the cameras caught that?" Tavi winced.

"The cameras catch everything," Alice said grimly. Then she told them the most important part of the story: Phyllis's pigeon pie catastrophe.

Henry took notes throughout, humming now and then. "Sounds like it could be sabotage," he concluded when Alice had finished.

"I thought so too," she said. "But I don't see how someone could have poured oil over Phyllis's oven mitts. I watched the whole challenge, and I didn't see anything like that. But I thought it was worth investigating."

"It definitely is," said Henry. "Maybe the saboteur greased Phyllis's oven mitts before the competition started. She probably wouldn't have used them early on, right?"

Alice agreed this was a possibility.

"Mysterious," said Tavi.

"Exactly." Henry's eyes shone. "It's a mystery."

"Oh!" Tavi snapped her fingers. "What if it's a poltergeist?"

He sighed. "Would you stop it with the ghosts? This is a human at work."

"How do you know?"

He looked irritated. "I just know. And what's more, we're going to prove it."

"We are?" said Alice.

He nodded. "If there's a saboteur at work on the set of *Culinary Combat*, we're going to find them."

"And unmask them!" added Tavi.

"Oh. Okay," Alice agreed, although unmasking a saboteur sounded more than a little terrifying. But if someone was sabotaging the competition, they absolutely had to be stopped.

"First we need to make a list." Henry turned to Alice. "So, who are our suspects?"

She opened her mouth, then closed it. She had no idea.

"Go with your instincts," he advised. "Just say the first name that comes to mind."

"Okay." She drew a breath. "Tom Truffleman."

"Hmm!" He noted this in his book. "Why?"

"Well, he's really mean."

"He's awful," Tavi agreed. "I saw an episode of *Bare-knuckled Bakers* where he made every single baker cry."

"Okay, so he's a jerk," said Henry. "But what's his motive? Why would he sabotage the contestants on his own show?"

"To create more drama?" Tavi suggested.

Alice shivered. If Tom Truffleman was sabotaging the competitors to make the show more dramatic, he was worse than mean. He was *despicable*.

Henry added a star next to his name. "We'll call him the Prime Suspect. Or the 'PS' if we ever need to keep it on the DL."

"Sorry?" Tavi looked confused.

"The down-low," Alice explained, glad that piece of information had finally come in handy. "It means to keep things quiet."

Henry nodded approvingly. "We might need to speak in code if we're in public."

"PS on the DL." Tavi nodded. "Got it."

"Okay, who else?" asked Henry. "We need to consider more than one suspect."

"How about that producer you mentioned?" Tavi suggested. "She might want to create drama too."

"Jasmina?" Alice tried to picture her secretly pouring oil over Phyllis's oven mitts. But she couldn't; Jasmina always seemed exhausted by the whole production.

"I'll add her to the list anyway," Henry said. "Who else?"

"What about Miranda Summers? She's the new host," Alice told Henry.

"Oh, I know." He added her to the list. "But what's her motive?"

Alice wasn't sure. "She just doesn't belong, you know? I don't think she cares about cooking at all."

"Why did they hire her, then?" asked Tavi.

Alice shrugged. "She's been on reality TV shows, like —"

"She got her start as a contestant on *Eligible*," Henry cut in. "Then she interned on *Match Made in Hollywood* before hosting *Why Are You Wearing That?* and its spin-off series *What Were You Thinking When You Got That Haircut?*"

Tavi blinked at him. "And you keep *that* information in your brain attic?"

"It could be important data!" he retorted, his ears turning pink. "Anyway, what's her motive?"

Alice thought hard but couldn't come up with anything. They concluded that more research was necessary.

"What about the contestants who lost the first two challenges?" said Tavi. "What if one of them wanted revenge?"

"They both left right away," Alice told her. François, of course, was somewhere in Belize, and according to Tina, Diana's parents had picked her up a few hours after the salted jelly disaster.

"Well, this is a pretty good list to start with," Henry said.

"Yeah, but we're forgetting one suspect," said Tavi.

They turned to her.

"*The poltergeist.*"

"Oh, come *on*," Henry groaned.

She held up a hand. "Hear me out. Who else — or *what* else — could sneak into the Great Hall and pour oil over someone's oven mitts without anyone noticing? Think about it. You'd have to be invisible!"

Alice agreed it would be helpful. But a poltergeist?

"Let's just consider it, okay?" said Tavi. "It's a possibility to rule out. That's what Sherlock Holmes would do," she added.

"Sherlock Holmes did *not* believe in ghosts!" Henry retorted.

"And that's why you're an even better detective." She patted his arm. "You consider all the possibilities."

Henry began to protest, then stopped, looking perplexed.

"So, here's an idea," Tavi hurried on. "Tonight, we'll investigate. Tonight, we'll rule out the possibility of a poltergeist at work."

"How?" asked Alice.

"I'm glad you asked." She grinned. "There just happens to be a séance . . ."

"*Not* a séance." Henry smacked his forehead.

"Isn't that where —"

"We'll get to commune with the ghosts of Gladstone Manor!" Tavi finished. "There'll be a medium who'll talk to them, and we'll get her to ask them questions. It's going to be great."

"This sounds like a terrible way to gather evidence," Henry grumbled.

"But fun, right?" Tavi looked at Henry, who shook his head. She looked to Alice. "Fun?"

Alice swallowed hard. "I mean, I guess it would help us rule out one suspect . . ."

"You've got to be kidding me," said Henry.

"You consider all the possibilities, remember?" Tavi said. "It's what makes you a great detective."

"I didn't say that — you did," he grunted.

"Just one séance," she insisted. "And if we can't find any evidence, we'll strike the ghost off the suspect list. Okay?"

Henry hesitated. "And you promise you'll let it go?"

"Promise."

He didn't look convinced, but he relented on the condition that they never tell anyone that he'd gone to a séance.

"Your secret's safe with us, Detective Oh," Tavi promised. "We'll keep it on the DL."

After the meeting, Alice headed for her father's room, still sifting through potential suspects in her mind. She dug her key out of her pocket and let herself in, not sure whether he would be there, or what she'd say to him if he was. All she knew was that she needed a change of clothes. And probably a shower.

"Hello?" she called as she slipped off her sneakers. No one answered. She showered quickly, then changed her clothes and swapped the cookbook in her backpack for a different one.

Her father arrived just as she was re-braiding her hair in front of the mirror over the fireplace.

"Alice!" His face brightened, then darkened just as quickly. "If only you could have helped me with that challenge today."

"Oh." She let the braid fall from her fingers. "Yeah."

"Yeah." He kicked off his shoes. "I'm sorry, sous-chef. I let us both down." He sank down on the sofa. "It didn't help that my lucky scarf is missing. You haven't seen it, have you?"

She shook her head, trying to think of something encouraging to say. "It wasn't . . . that bad. I mean, at least you didn't drop your pie."

He sighed. "Poor Phyllis. She's already left the manor, and she swears she'll never cook competitively again."

"I don't blame her." Alice finished her braid and tossed it over her shoulder.

"Where did you go after filming? You left so quickly."

"I had to meet Tavi and Henry."

"How come?"

She tried to imagine what he'd do if she told him they were searching for a saboteur. He'd probably worry. And he'd definitely demand an explanation. Once again, it seemed best to keep the whole thing on the down-low.

"We had plans to eat breakfast together," she said. "I mean lunch. I was super hungry."

"Of course," he said, then sighed again. "I really wish they had let you cook today. And not just because you could have braided that darn dough with your eyes closed, but . . . well, it just didn't feel right without you."

She was glad to hear it. "It was hard to watch from off set."

"I can imagine. You must have wanted to rip the dough out of my hands and braid it yourself. You must have been going crazy!"

"A little," she admitted.

"Stupid braided lattice." He shook his head. "At least next time we get to cook together. I think we need that, don't you?"

She agreed. And it was such a relief not to be fighting anymore that she actually smiled and sat down beside him. "It'll be like old times."

He smiled back. "And best of all, we get a rest day tomorrow! I definitely need that." He pointed to her backpack. "Are you moving back in?"

"Oh. Um, I wasn't planning to."

"Your sleepover was a success, then?"

She nodded. "I like staying with Tavi." And with all the investigating they planned to do, it made sense for her stay in the kids' corner of the manor.

"I'm glad. And I'm proud of you." He dropped a kiss on her forehead. "And now, Alice, we need to talk about Hana."

She felt like a soufflé collapsing, left in the oven too long. Why did he have to ruin a perfectly good moment by bringing up Hana?

"I know you don't want to talk about her, but it's important to me, and to Hana too. I just want you to give her a chance, Alice. She's a lot like you, you know: you're both smart and kind and funny. I'd say you have the same sense of humor."

Alice hadn't seen any indication of Hana having a sense of humor, but she kept that to herself.

"Look, I know you were annoyed to find out we were dating," he went on, "And I'm sorry I didn't tell you sooner, but I needed time to get used to it myself. This relationship is very new for me too, Alice. I didn't want to introduce anyone into our lives until I was sure. I know you'd like Hana if you gave her a chance. I want you to like her."

I don't want to like her, thought Alice, but she kept that to herself too.

"So, what do you say?"

She didn't know what to say.

She wished she had Tavi there to counsel her. What would Tavi say? Alice pictured her friend, fingers tented below her chin, advising Alice to take some time away from everything that was bothering her. "Me-time" she'd called it.

And maybe that was it.

"I need time too," she said.

"I'm sorry?"

"You took time to get used to Hana before you introduced me to her. You just said so."

"Well, not so much Hana as the relation —"

"*So*," she cut in, "I need to take time too. To get used to her." *Or not*, she added to herself. Maybe she never would.

"Alice, I don't think that's the same —"

"That is what I need," she told him, channeling Tavi's calm and confidence.

He raised a ginger eyebrow, then shrugged. "All right, then. If that's what you need. I suppose it's only fair."

"It is," she agreed. "Now, I have to go. I'm hanging out with Tavi for the rest of the day." She zipped up her backpack and slipped it on her shoulder.

"Where are you going now?"

She wasn't about to tell him the truth: that they'd be preparing to commune with the manor's ghosts, seeking evidence of a saboteur. "Going to see the exhibit in the ballroom," she said. "I hear it's good."

She'd never kept secrets from her father before. And she'd never imagined it would be so easy.

CHAPTER
15

They spent the afternoon in Tavi's room, watching *Desserts to Die For* on her tablet and snacking on the chocolate bars she kept in her suitcase. She'd learned to bring a stash to every historical reenactment festival, "Because you never know with historically accurate food."

Alice understood this completely.

At seven o'clock that evening, they set off to the séance. Tavi was wearing the white dress again, and she'd paired it with a wide-brimmed hat trimmed with ostrich feathers. Henry had donned his deerstalker and carried his notebook, as usual. Alice, meanwhile, wore shorts, a T-shirt and sneakers. Tavi had offered to help her find a more séance-appropriate outfit, but Alice had declined. For one thing, she'd never been a fan of dresses, and even the simplest Victorian frocks looked far too frilly for her. But, more importantly, on the off chance that they actually met a ghost, she wanted to be ready to run.

The séance was being held on the third floor, a few doors down from the Bartitsu classroom, the sight of which still made Alice cringe. They found the door ajar, so they stepped inside and looked around a dimly lit room about the size of Tavi's. A big, round table draped in black cloth stood in the center; a cloudy lantern on top of it cast the only light. Alice could just make out a bookshelf on one wall and an armchair beside it.

"Creepy," she murmured.

"Totally," Tavi said happily.

"It's all just for show," Henry scoffed.

"Hello," someone said, and they all jumped. They hadn't noticed the woman sitting at the table. Her black hair was piled atop her head, and she wore a large brooch at her throat that appeared to be adorned with hair, the strands woven together like a lattice-top pie. Alice recoiled.

"Oh, hi!" said Tavi. "We're here for the séance. I'm Tavi." She shook the woman's hand, then introduced Alice and Henry.

"I'm Veronica." The woman motioned for them all to take a seat. "I'll be your medium this evening. A medium," she added, "is someone who can speak to ghosts. Think of me as a channel to the afterlife."

"Oh, we know," Tavi assured her, pulling up a chair. "Hey, while we're waiting, can you tell me a bit about the medium business? Like, how'd you get into it? And is this your full-time job? Or more of a side hustle?"

While Tavi interviewed the medium, Henry looked around the room, making notes in his book. Alice sat quietly beside them, marveling at how they weren't the least bit embarrassed about their peculiar obsessions. She felt a twinge of envy, watching them being so completely, comfortably themselves.

Soon they were joined by four adults: two men in sharp suits and pointy shoes and two women in hats that looked a bit like birthday presents, festooned with ribbons and bows. They took their seats at the table, chattering about a session they'd attended that afternoon that seemed to have involved hunting for ferns.

"Did you say ferns?" Tavi cut in.

One of the women nodded excitedly. "It was a session on pteridomania — that means an obsession with ferns. The Victorians were *so* into ferns."

"We spent the afternoon hunting for them in the forest," one of the men added. "Then we pressed our collections between sheets of parchment paper to dry them out. It was incredible."

It sounded far from *incredible* to Alice, but she smiled politely.

"I should have been born in the Victorian age." The other woman straightened her hat. "I documented the afternoon on PHOMO. Want to see?" She held up her phone.

"Ooh, yes, please." Tavi leaned across the table.

But Veronica the medium cleared her throat. "No phones are allowed at the séance. I'll have to ask you to turn them off."

"No phones at all?" The woman looked shocked, and Alice wondered if she knew that had she been born in the Victorian age, she wouldn't be documenting her pteridomania on PHOMO.

Veronica shook her head.

Clearly disappointed, the adults put away their phones.

"Well, then, let's begin," said Veronica. "I hope you're all ready for an otherworldly experience, one you won't soon forget. For those of you I haven't met, I am Veronica, and I have been trained in the art and science of speaking with the dead."

"Science," Henry huffed. Alice elbowed him.

"The process is simple. I will invite a ghost into the room, and when it arrives, you will have the opportunity to ask it questions. The ghost will speak through me, so don't be alarmed if I don't sound like myself. Also," she cleared her throat, "I have a bit of a cold."

"This is so great," Tavi whispered.

147

Alice only hoped it would be over quickly. She couldn't help but stare at Veronica's brooch. Was it her own hair woven into the lattice? Or someone else's? And which was worse?

The medium took a long, deep breath, then closed her eyes. "Is anyone out there?" she called. "Come closer if you are."

In the pause that followed, Alice thought she felt a light breeze tickle the back of her neck. "Henry, stop it," she hissed.

"Stop what?"

"Don't be frightened," said Veronica. "These fine guests would like to speak to you. They want to know your story."

Alice felt the breeze again. She glanced around for an open window, but they all appeared to be covered by heavy curtains. Then she heard a whistling sound from over near the book-case. She was just about to turn when Veronica gasped and reeled, as if someone had just hit her. One of the men yelped.

The medium opened her eyes and blinked at the guests around the table. When she spoke, her voice was low and grumbly. "*I am heeere.*"

"Yessss!" Tavi whisper-cheered.

"Oh, come on," said Henry.

"*What do you want?*" the medium growled.

The adults exchanged glances. "What do we do now?" one man whispered.

"Ask it something," said the other.

"Um . . . who are you?" asked one of the women.

The medium drew a ragged breath. "*I am . . . Ignatius Silverbottom. I lived in this manor for fifty years.*"

"Fifty years, huh?" Henry noted this, then leaned forward, crossing his arms on the table. "Okay, Silverbottom, if that is your name. So, how did you die?"

"Henry!" Tavi elbowed him.

"What? We need to know."

"*I died from . . . a broken heaaart,*" the medium rasped.

"Awww," the adults cooed.

"Not sure that can actually happen, but okay." Henry jotted it down.

"Could you tell us about your true love —" one of the men began.

But Henry cut in. "More importantly, have you seen anything strange in the manor lately?"

"Henry!" Tavi widened her eyes at him. "*Rude.*"

The medium blinked at him. "*Strange?*"

He nodded.

"*There are always strange things going on at Gladstone Manor.*"

"Uh-huh." Henry raised an eyebrow. "Maybe you can be more specific?"

"He's not just going to come out and admit to sabotage," Tavi whispered.

"You ask him a question, then! Or Alice."

"No, you." Alice gestured to Tavi.

"Can I ask a question?" one of the men ventured.

"Just a sec." Tavi cleared her throat. "Mr. Silverbottom, have you been to the Great Hall lately? Like, where *Culinary Combat* is being filmed?"

The medium's eyes widened. "*How dare they!*" She thumped the table with her fist, making everyone jump.

"Whoa." Alice gripped her chair as the breeze swept through the room again and the lantern flickered on the table. Henry must have felt it too, because he straightened and looked around.

"This is actually kind of creepy," one of the men muttered.

But the medium was just getting going. *"How dare they film a television show in the Great Hall of Gladstone Manor? It is a place of ceremony!"* She thumped the table again. *"And circumstance!"*

"See? He's upset about it!" Tavi hissed. "Alice, your turn. Ask him about the sabotage."

"Me? Oh." Alice let go of her chair and laced her fingers together in her lap. "Okay. Mr. . . . Silverbottom, sir, I'm wondering if you might have . . . I mean, we're not accusing you of anything. But . . . well, did you ever consider —"

"Did you sabotage the cooking show?" Henry cut in. "Like, for real. Did you shut off someone's oven while they were baking a cake? Or pour oil over someone else's oven mitts?"

"What is with these kids?" wondered one of the women.

"Henry, he's not just going to come out and say it!" Tavi argued.

"No, he's not." Henry stood up and pushed back his chair. "You know why? Because he isn't real. Isn't that right, Leo?"

"Leo?" said Alice.

"Leo?" echoed the guests.

"Sorry, what?" said a muffled voice that seemed to come from the bookshelf.

Henry reached over and flicked a light switch on the wall, illuminating the room.

"Hey!" Veronica shouted. "What are you doing?"

"This." He marched to the bookshelf and gave it a shove. It rolled easily, revealing an open door behind it.

And a man in the doorway, holding a wireless fan and a slide whistle.

It was Leo, Hana's Bartitsu assistant.

"Oh, hi everyone." He waved. The whistle dropped from his hand and clattered to the floor. "I'm . . . um . . . here."

"Definitely not a ghost," Henry said smugly.

"What?" cried Tavi.

"Leo!" Veronica groaned.

"Hey, it's not my fault the kid figured it out. How did you do that, anyway?" Leo asked.

But Henry was busy inspecting the room where Leo had been hiding. "A secret room, huh?" he murmured. "Now *that's* interesting."

"I knew it was a hoax all along," one of the men said.

"You were *trembling*," the other pointed out.

"Hey, look on the bright side," Leo suggested. "In Victorian times, some scam artists would charge people a lot of money for this. You guys got a fake séance for free!"

"Not helping, Leo," Veronica grumbled. "Also, I'm not a scam artist. I'm an *actor*."

He shrugged. "Well, you can see how easy it was for the Victorians to fall for this kind of thing."

"We didn't fall for it," Henry called from the secret room.

Alice looked over at Tavi, who looked a bit deflated. She patted her shoulder. "I mostly fell for it."

Tavi nodded. "I did too. Mostly."

While the adults asked Veronica about her acting career, Tavi and Alice joined Henry in the secret room.

"How did you know Leo was in here?" Alice peered inside to find a dark, empty space, roughly the size of a bathroom.

"It's elementary!" Henry raised a finger in the air. When Tavi and Alice stared at him, he shrugged. "I heard his ringtone."

"His *ringtone*?"

"Like, on his phone?" said Tavi.

Henry nodded. "It's the theme song for the Sherlock Holmes miniseries. I heard it once during Bartitsu practice, so when it went off while Veronica was talking, I knew he was here. I wasn't sure where he was hiding, but I figured if I shouted his name, he'd answer." He shrugged. "He just seemed like that kind of person."

"His ringtone," Alice repeated, incredulous. "I didn't even hear it."

"Good detectives are always listening," Henry told her. "That's why I'm an expert eavesdropper."

"That's pretty impressive," said Tavi. "It almost makes up for the fact that we didn't find a poltergeist."

"Oh, it totally does," said Henry. "And not just because it was a brilliant piece of detective work. We found this." He gestured to the room. "Maybe it was once a closet?"

"Do you think there might be more rooms like this?" asked Alice.

"Maybe." He grinned.

"Super cool," said Tavi. "So, just to be clear, Henry, you're pretty glad you came to the séance, aren't you?"

He rolled his eyes but had to admit it was a productive use of his time.

"So, what's next?" Alice asked after they'd said goodbye to Veronica and Leo and stepped back out into the hallway.

"We've got a lot of inspecting to do." Henry pulled down the brim of his hat. "And a solid list of suspects."

"Let's spend tomorrow researching," said Tavi. "You've got the day off, right, Alice?"

Alice nodded. Day Five of the competition was a rest day.

They split up their list of suspects: Tavi took Miranda, and Henry wanted to spy on Tom Truffleman, which left Alice with Jasmina. They agreed to spend the morning researching, then meet up later in the day and share their findings.

"Keep an eye out for other potential suspects too," Henry advised as they parted ways for the night.

"And secret rooms," Alice added.

"And ghosts," said Tavi. "Just for fun!" she added when Henry began to protest. "I'm never going to stop looking for ghosts, you know. That would be like . . . like you giving up detective work, or Alice giving up cooking. The heart wants what the heart wants, right?"

Even Henry couldn't argue with this.

The heart wants what the heart wants, Alice repeated to herself as she changed into her pajamas and climbed into bed. Until *Culinary Combat* had begun, her heart had always wanted to cook. Now she could think of a hundred things she'd rather do.

And that made her heart hurt.

The next morning, Alice's phone buzzed, at long last, with a message from Mat.

I have a new PHOMO account for my art! he said. It's @Matzcreationz. I wanna get lots of followers and be an influencer — that's my new plan for surviving middle school. Way better than learning jiu-jitsu, right??

Alice read the message three times, then looked over at Tavi. "What's an 'influencer'?" They were both still in pajamas, and still in bed, though it was now mid-morning.

"A big deal on social media," Tavi explained, without looking up from her own phone. "Influencers have loads of followers, so they have, well, influence. Sometimes companies pay them to promote their products."

"Oh." Alice read the message again, wondering what this would mean for her friendship with Mat. She didn't like the sound of it.

"There are a few influencers at my school," Tavi went on. "One guy choreographed a dance that went viral — you know, this one?" She waved her hands in front of her face, then swung them around her head and punched the air. "That's how it starts."

Alice shook her head.

"Anyway, he became crazy popular overnight."

"I guess that's what Mat's hoping for," said Alice. "It's his strategy for surviving middle school. His sister Cami told him he needed one, because anything can happen in middle school. Is that . . . true?"

Tavi frowned. "Anything like what?"

Alice shrugged. She hadn't asked Cami for details, but she'd once seen a kid get stuffed in a locker on a TV show, so she'd been picturing something along those lines.

"You're not worried, are you, Alice? You look worried."

"Maybe . . . a little," she admitted. "I don't have a survival strategy yet. I've just been trying not to think about it." And whenever she did, she felt sick to her stomach.

Tavi waved this away. "All you need to do is show up and be yourself. I know that sounds cheesy, but it's true. That's the best strategy. Actually, I think it's the only strategy."

It didn't sound like much of a strategy to Alice. In fact, it sounded downright dangerous.

"Look, Alice." Tavi propped herself up on one elbow. "If you can survive even one *Culinary Combat* challenge with Tom Truffleman, you can deal with middle school. I promise."

This reminded Alice of her greatest fear: what the other kids would think if they recognized her from the show. She was about to ask Tavi whether she thought this was likely to happen, and if so whether she ought to find a disguise, or maybe dye her hair. But then someone knocked at the door.

"I'll bet that's my mom," Tavi said, rolling out of bed. "She probably wants to know how the séance went. My mom loves a good — Oh!" she said as she opened the door. "Hi!"

"Hi, Octavia. I'm Alice's father."

Alice sat up as James stepped into the room, immediately noting the wrinkle between his eyebrows. "What's wrong?"

"I hate to tell you this," he said, "but they changed the rules again."

"They *what?*"

He sighed. "*Culinary Combat.* It's today. In fact, it's now."

"Now?" She flung off the covers. "Not tomorrow? It's supposed to be tomorrow!"

"I know. Hana and I were just sitting down to a nice breakfast when Jasmina came and broke the news. Tom Truffleman decided to take away our rest day. We have to report to the Great Hall right now."

"Truffleman again!" Tavi cried. "That guy's the worst!"

"You're not wrong." James turned back to Alice. "Sorry, sous-chef. On the bright side, it seems like all the assistants are allowed to compete today."

"But . . ." She looked down at her pajamas, then around the room. She wasn't prepared at all. She hadn't read a cookbook in days. She didn't even have clean clothes to wear!

"Here." He held out a bundle of her clothes. "I thought you might want some." Then he stepped out into the hallway while she changed.

She dressed as quickly as possible, while Tavi sat on the fainting couch and tried to put a curse on Tom Truffleman and all his descendants. Alice half listened while wondering what awaited them in the Great Hall. Her heart began to pound.

"I'm not sure the curse worked," Tavi said as Alice headed for the door, still braiding her hair. "But I tried." She gave her a good-luck hug.

James handed her a crumpet wrapped in a napkin, which

she ate as they hustled down the stairs and across the lobby to the Great Hall. This time, the doors were open, so they hurried right in.

They stopped at the sight of the workstations. There were six of them . . . but only three teams left in the competition.

"Wait, why six?" Alice asked over a mouthful of crumpet.

"Oh no," James gulped.

"What do you mean, *oh no*? What's going — *Oh no!*" she said as she realized. "Dad! They aren't going to make us —"

"James! Alice!" Jasmina beckoned them across the hall to where she stood with the other competitors. Samir looked stricken. Toni looked as though she wanted to wring someone's neck.

Tom Truffleman, Jasmina explained, had decided that for this challenge each team would be split up. Every competitor would cook alone at their own station.

"Competing *against* their partners!" Samir folded his arms across his chest.

"No!" Alice breathed.

James put a hand on her shoulder. "Is this really necessary?" he asked Jasmina.

She shrugged miserably. "There's nothing I can do."

Alice looked around at the video cameras and lights and crew members darting every which way. "I can't do this by myself," she said.

"Oh, sous-chef." James looked even more miserable than Jasmina. "I'm so sorry."

And he couldn't help her, Alice realized. It made her want to throw up.

"Now that's not fair," Toni declared. "Alice shouldn't have to compete by herself. She's a child!"

Jasmina looked left, then right, then crouched down in front of Alice. "Are you okay with this?"

Alice tried to swallow the lump in her throat. "Not really, no."

"Right. Because . . ." Jasmina lowered her voice. "I mean, you *could* say no."

"I could?" She hadn't expected that. "What would happen then?"

"I'm not sure, to be honest. You'd be breaking your contract. But no one can force you to cook if you really don't want to. Not even Tom Truffleman."

Alice tried to imagine what the judge would do if she refused to cook alone. Would he be angry? Or would he claim he'd been right all along — that a kid should never have been allowed on his show?

She recalled the third challenge, when he'd scolded her father for relying on a twelve-year-old girl. And the second challenge, when he'd congratulated James and ignored her completely. And the first challenge, when he'd declared outright that kids couldn't cook.

Thinking about it made her neck prickle and her fists clench. She didn't want to cook alone. But she definitely didn't want to prove him right.

"I think . . . I'm going to compete," she said.

"You are?" said Jasmina.

"You *are*?" echoed the twins, who'd been hovering nearby.

"Yes," she said, hoping she wasn't making a huge mistake. "I think so." She looked to her father, who nodded, though the wrinkle between his eyebrows was bigger than ever.

"Great!" Jasmina swept Alice over to her workstation, right at the front of the row. It felt very large and lonely without her father beside her. She slipped on her apron while someone fastened a microphone to her collar.

"I'm right here if you need me," James called from the station behind hers.

"Us too," the twins added from their stations across the aisle. "Let us know if we can help."

"Technically, you're not allowed to help each other," Jasmina told them. "Tom wants to see every competitor working alone. *But*," she added quietly, "I think you should do whatever you need to. Just keep it on the down-low."

Alice nodded. That she could do.

Tom Truffleman and Miranda Summers arrived shortly before the filming began. They stopped and looked around, and Alice felt their eyes linger on her. She looked down at her hands, willing them to stop shaking.

"Three minutes till we roll!" called Jasmina.

Miranda took her place at the front of the hall. Just before the cameras began rolling, she turned to Alice. "I could never do what you're doing," she said.

Alice looked up in surprise. "Why not?"

"Well, first off, I can't cook," the host admitted. "I once burned a pot while I was trying to boil water. After that I gave up trying. But also, I'd crack under the pressure of this competition. You're really brave, Alice." She gave her a small smile, then turned back to the cameras.

"Um, thanks."

Alice had never thought of herself as brave. She wasn't sure it was accurate, either. But there was no time to think about it, because now the cameras were rolling and Miranda was announcing that today each of the competitors would be making . . .

"A charlotte russe!"

Alice's jaw dropped. *A charlotte russe?*

"A what?" Toni looked at her sister, panicked. "I don't know what that is!"

"Me neither," said Samir.

"The charlotte russe has many different components, and you'll have to make them all from scratch. This is one complicated dessert," Miranda warned, and for once, she sounded genuinely concerned.

Alice nodded dumbly. When she was eight years old, she and her father had made a charlotte russe together. It had taken an entire day.

"You have three and a half hours," Miranda told them. "Good luck."

CHAPTER 17

"Just take one thing at a time," James murmured. "Slow and steady, sous-chef."

Alice felt anything but steady. Her head was spinning as she tried to recall all the parts of a charlotte russe. She knew she'd have to make a creamy, custardy filling called a bavarois. And ladyfinger cookies too — those would stand vertically around the edge of the dessert. She was fairly certain it needed a fruit jelly topping, and it definitely had to chill in the freezer for as long as possible or else the whole thing would be an oozing mess.

It was, as Miranda had said, one complicated dessert

Her heart hammered as she looked around the room. How would she manage?

"You have a recipe," James whispered.

"Right." She pulled it out of her drawer, blinked hard and read it through.

As far as she could tell, all the ingredients were listed, along with instructions for making the bavarois, ladyfingers and jelly topping. What the recipe lacked was instructions for putting it all together. She dimly remember James calling it a "feat of engineering," and having to look up what that meant.

It meant it was hard to construct . . . and easy to mess up.

By the time she looked up again, Tina and Sven were collecting their ingredients from the shelves. Toni and Samir were still hunched over their recipes, their heads in their hands. Alice felt the urge to hold her head in her hands too, or maybe crawl into a cupboard and never emerge. But she forced herself to stay upright and take deep breaths.

One thing at a time, she told herself. First, she had to bake the ladyfinger cookies, since they would need time to cool. She took her recipe over to the shelves, where her father was waiting.

"You all right?" he whispered.

She didn't know how to answer, so she didn't try.

"I'll help you —" he began.

But Tom Truffleman popped up beside them, wagging a finger. "No helping. Today it's every cook for themselves."

James muttered a curse word — either he'd forgotten about his microphone or simply didn't care.

Alice turned her back on them both and focused on her ingredients. Once she'd gathered them all, she returned to her station, aware of a video camera trailing her but trying hard to pretend it didn't exist. Her only job, she told herself, was to make a charlotte russe, or at least something resembling it.

You don't have to care about the cameras.

She repeated this to herself three times. Then she began to bake.

"One thing at a time," she whispered as she separated the egg yolks from the whites. "One thing at a time," as she whisked the yolks and sugar together until they turned pale and creamy. "One thing at a time," as she added vanilla and breathed in the

162

smell, which was one of her very favorites. She folded her dry ingredients into the egg yolk mixture, then whisked the egg whites, some sugar and cream of tartar into a glossy meringue and incorporated that as well.

The funny thing about ladyfingers, she knew, was that you couldn't just spoon the dough onto a cookie sheet and bake. They had to look like long, fat fingers, and for that you needed a piping bag. She found one in a drawer, then carefully filled it with her cookie mixture and began to squeeze it onto the baking sheet.

She was so focused that she didn't notice Tom Truffleman standing beside her until he cleared his throat. She jumped, and the nozzle of her piping bag sank right into a cookie.

"Never made these before, have you?" he sniffed.

"I have," she said shortly. She hadn't made them *by herself*, but she didn't need to tell him that. In fact, she didn't need to tell him anything. She turned away from the judge and piped another cookie.

He harrumphed. "Well then, you must know that you need to make them all the same size."

She looked up and glanced around the room. Across the aisle, Tina was using a ruler and pencil to mark the precise dimensions of each cookie on parchment paper. Behind her, Sven was doing the same.

"Shoot," she muttered as the judge sauntered off. She'd have to start again. Fortunately, she hadn't used up much of her mixture, but she'd have to be careful not to waste what she had left. She grabbed a clean cookie sheet, lined it with parchment paper, then got to work measuring, marking and piping.

By the time she slid her baking sheet into the oven and set the timer, she was exhausted. According to the clock on the wall, forty-five minutes had already passed, and she still had to make a bavarois and a jelly topping, then assemble the cake *and* let it chill.

"I can't do this," she whispered.

"One thing at a time," James reminded her.

"I *can't*," she insisted, and her eyes began to sting.

Miranda appeared beside her with a big glass of water. "Here." She thrust it into Alice's hands. "Drink this. Water is very calming, you know. It also does wonders for the skin. Drink lots now, and you'll thank me in the future."

Alice took a big gulp of water and felt a little bit better. She thanked Miranda, then she went back to the shelves to collect ingredients for her bavarois.

When she returned, the host was chatting with James. "It must be so hard for you to watch her going through this alone," she was saying.

"Unbelievably hard," he agreed as he cracked eggs into a bowl. "But Alice is a very good cook."

"But she's just a child!" Miranda insisted. "Don't you think it's too much for her?"

"It's a lot," he said. "But children can do great things. Contrary to what some people think, they really *can* cook."

Alice sneaked a glance at Tom Truffleman, wondering if he'd caught that. But he was busy counting the flaws in Samir's ladyfingers.

"Have you ever heard of Marie-Antoine Carême?" James asked Miranda.

"No! She sounds fancy."

"Well, Carême was a boy," James told her. "And he's considered by many to be the world's first celebrity chef."

Miranda leaned against his workstation. "Tell me more!"

Alice listened as she began to prepare her bavarois, first heating milk in a pan on the stove, then whisking together some egg yolks and sugar.

"Carême was born in Paris in the 1780s," James began. "The sixteenth child in a very poor family, he was abandoned by his parents when he was still just a boy, during the French Revolution."

Miranda tsked. "So sad."

"At age eight, he was working as a kitchen boy in a restaurant in exchange for food and shelter. He worked extremely hard, and by the time he was fifteen he was an apprentice to a famous pastry chef, who also taught him to read and write. Carême would spend hours at the library reading books on art and architecture, which served to inspire him in the kitchen. He began to create elaborate pastry sculptures of the things he read about: temples, pyramids, ancient ruins. They were so stunning that people would travel from far and wide to see these incredible pastry sculptures."

Alice paused to imagine Carême's sculptures, wondering what kind of pastry he'd used to make them. She made a mental note to find out.

"He invented many famous desserts as well," James went on. "Like the mille-feuille and the charlotte russe."

"You mean . . . ?" Miranda waved her hand around.

James nodded. "He cooked for royalty too — I believe he even designed Napoleon's wedding cake. And he wrote cookbooks, attempting to make fine cooking accessible to everyday people. So, it just goes to show you," he concluded, "children can do great things."

Tina appeared at Alice's side and squeezed her shoulder. "And it looks like this one just made a beautiful bavarois."

It was true: the cream she'd whipped up while listening to James was perfectly thick and smooth. Now all she had to do was make a jelly topping and —

Tina sniffed. "Is something burning?"

Alice crouched to check on her ladyfingers in the oven. They were browning nicely, but not burning. She inhaled deeply, then spun around. "Dad! Your saucepan!"

He yelped, then swiped the smoking saucepan off his stovetop and dumped it in the sink. "What is the matter with this stove?" he cried. "I have the temperature on low, but it still gets so hot!" He rubbed his temples. "Thank you, Alice. You just saved me from burning down Gladstone Manor."

"I have space on my stove, James," Samir offered. "If yours is glitchy, feel free to use mine."

Alice wondered if Tom Truffleman would protest, since helping wasn't allowed. But the judge was nowhere to be seen. James quickly remade the jelly topping he'd burned, then set it on Samir's stove to cook.

Alice took her ladyfingers out of the oven and let them cool alongside her bavarois. Then she began to assemble her dessert, trying her best to recall how she and her father had done it four years before. First, she lined a springform cake tin with parchment paper, then she stood her ladyfinger cookies vertically, side by side, around the inside edge of the tin. Next, she spooned the bavarois into the tin, then quickly put the dish in a fridge to chill.

Now she had to make a topping like the one her father had burned. She grabbed a pint of fresh raspberries from the fridge and boiled them with some sugar and a few leaves of gelatin. Once the cake was suitably cold, she would pour the topping over it, then put it back in the fridge for as long as possible and hope that it would set.

With just half an hour left in the challenge, Alice poured raspberry jelly over her cake, then tucked it back in the fridge. But just as she was headed back to her workstation, she heard Samir gasp, "Oh no!" He was standing at his station with a saucepan in one hand, a spoon in the other and a look of alarm on his face.

"What now?" asked Sven.

Samir looked down at the pot, then over at James. "Um . . . James, I think you took my saucepan."

James looked up from the cake he'd just finished topping. "Sorry, what?"

Samir nodded. "My raspberry topping was right next to your strawberry. When you took yours back, you must have . . ."

James's spoon clattered to the floor. "Samir, I'm so sorry! I had no idea!"

"I'm sure you didn't," Samir said ruefully.

"Oh *no!*" James tore at his hair. "I can't believe I did that!"

"Did what?" Tom Truffleman swooped in like a detective at the scene of a crime. "James, did I hear correctly? Did you swipe Samir's saucepan?"

"I did," James moaned. "I got them mixed up."

"And why were you using his stove?" the judge demanded.

"Because mine is glitchy," he explained. "The elements stay hot even when the temperature's on low. I have no idea why."

"Is that so?" Truffleman's eyes narrowed. "You know, James, we cannot tolerate cheating on *Culinary Combat.*"

"Cheating?" James cried.

"Cheating?" Alice echoed.

"I'm sure it was an accident," said Samir.

"Well, I'm not," huffed Truffleman.

"How *dare* you!" Toni bustled over, wielding a spatula. "James is not a cheater!"

"No, he is not!" Alice added, but her voice was lost in the commotion, for now every videographer was hustling over to catch the drama. Was this what they wanted? she wondered, watching them circle James's station like hungry piranhas.

Then another question came to mind. Had someone done this *on purpose*? Was it once again the work of the saboteur?

"All right, everyone." Jasmina squeezed into the crowd of cameras and bickering contestants. When no one paid attention, she yelled, "Hey! *Listen!*"

They stopped and looked at her.

"You have ten minutes left. Finish your desserts as best as you can, and we'll deal with all this after." She nodded at James and Samir. "Okay?"

Reluctantly, everyone returned to their stations.

Alice's hands were trembling. She couldn't for the life of her remember what she had to do next.

"It's okay," James assured her. "Just keep going. Your dessert is waiting — in the fridge," he added, which was helpful since she'd forgotten where it was.

With only a few minutes to spare, she took the cake out of the fridge, then carefully unclasped the springform tin that was holding it all together and lifted the outer ring. The ladyfingers remained upright, like sentries guarding a raspberry-red lake.

Despite her measurements, the cookies had turned out to be different sizes, and the cake was distinctly lopsided. But it was definitely a charlotte russe. And she'd made it all by herself.

"You should be very proud," Tina told her from across the aisle.

Alice nodded. She knew she should. But all she felt was worry.

When Miranda announced that the time was up, she turned to look at her father's creation. It was the perfect charlotte russe: the ladyfingers were golden-brown and identical, and his topping (or rather Samir's) was smooth and shiny.

"Okay everyone." Jasmina marched on set and signaled for the cameras to stop rolling. "Here's what's going to happen. Tom will now judge all the desserts except Samir's and James's. We'll name a winner, but we won't send anyone home today — at least not until we look into what happened. We need to review the video footage and inspect James's stove. I'm sure it was a simple mistake," she added to James.

"It really was," he said.

"But we need to investigate. We'll look into it tomorrow and give you the rest day you didn't have today. Seriously this time, you'll get to rest," she promised. "Does that sound fair?"

"Too generous, if you ask me," Truffleman muttered. The contestants glared at him.

"I guess it's fair," said Samir.

"Fair enough," sighed James.

Alice disagreed, but she forced herself to stay quiet. The adults, she knew, wouldn't listen to her anyway.

Thankfully, she knew two people who would.

CHAPTER

18

They all agreed: it sounded like sabotage.

"The worst kind of sabotage." Tavi pointed her spoon at Alice before swirling it in her teacup. "Because whoever is doing this just made your dad look like the saboteur! And now he's going to get in trouble for it!" She thumped her fist on the table and their teacups rattled. "This time . . . it's personal."

"Detectives can't take things personally," Henry told her. "Also, keep your voice down." He tilted his head toward the table beside them, where some guests were nibbling on cucumber sandwiches and scones. Since it was raining outside, they'd retreated to the dining room, where afternoon tea was being served.

"What happened with the judging?" he asked Alice. "You never told us how it ended."

"Oh, right." She'd been so focused on the sabotage that she'd forgotten. She described Tom Truffleman's horror when he cut into Toni's dessert and it oozed all over the table. The same thing had happened to Sven, much to his embarrassment.

Tina's cake, however, was practically perfect: the filling was creamy, the topping shiny and smooth. She'd won the challenge, hands down.

"And what about you?" asked Henry.

"Passable," she said. That was what Tom Truffleman had called her cake.

"You did this *all by yourself?*" he'd asked when she'd presented her charlotte russe, with all the components intact.

Her ears had burned, but she'd managed to keep her head up and look the judge in the eye. "All of it."

"It's better than passable," James had told her once the challenge was finally over. "It's an absolute delight. I'm so proud of you, Alice." Then he'd excused himself, saying he needed to go take a nap. This worried her: her father never took naps.

Henry pushed his teacup aside and took out his notebook. "The saboteur strikes again," he murmured. "And now things are getting serious. We've only got a few more days to figure this out. In three days, everyone will have left the manor, including our saboteur."

"And there's only one more cooking challenge," Tavi said.

Alice nodded, though she couldn't believe it — the competition was almost over, and somehow she was still in it.

"I guess you didn't get to investigate Jasmina as a suspect?" Henry asked Alice.

She hadn't, and now she felt even more sure than ever that Jasmina was not the saboteur. She recounted how that morning the producer had suggested Alice break the rules and refuse to cook. "Would a saboteur do that?"

No one was sure.

"Well, I investigated our prime suspect," Henry said. "As much as I could, anyway. I couldn't get into his room."

"You actually tried?" said Tavi.

He nodded. "The door was locked, and before I could pick it, the cleaning staff arrived. They stayed in there forever — I think they were trying to make the pillows fluffier?" He shrugged. "So I did some online research instead. And I found an article called . . ." He consulted his notebook. "'Truffleman talks back: the infamous judge denies manufacturing drama on *Bareknuckled Bakers*.' Apparently, he'd been accused of unfairly manipulating the competition to make it more dramatic. But in this interview, he totally denies it. He said . . ." Henry checked his notes again. "'If you put cutthroat competitors in a high-pressure environment and give them a challenge beyond their capabilities, drama will naturally ensue. There's no need to manufacture it. Reality TV creates its own drama.'"

"But he's always manipulating the competition!" Alice protested. "He shrank our workstations, took away our rest day and made the teammates compete against each other!"

"I guess he doesn't think that's unfair," said Henry.

Alice huffed. "Well, it's totally unfair."

"What about you, Tavi? Did you investigate Miranda Summers?"

Tavi nodded. "I decided to go to the place where she probably spends most of her time."

"Her room?" asked Henry. Tavi shook her head.

"The spa down the road?" guessed Alice.

"Nope. PHOMO."

"PHOMO!" Alice hadn't considered the app as a tool for tracking criminals.

Tavi looked pleased with herself. "I remembered this news story about a thief who'd stolen thousands of dollars in jewelry, and the police found her because she was posting selfies wearing the jewels on PHOMO. Crazy, right?"

Alice nodded. "What did you find?"

"Unfortunately, not much. Miranda mostly posts skin-care and makeup advice — nothing about her personal life. And nothing very interesting."

"Good sleuthing anyway." Henry noted her findings in his book. "Oh, and I also talked to the lead camera person."

"You mean Meg?" said Alice.

"Yeah. She has access to all the video footage from the past week. If the saboteur was on set during a challenge — say, switching off François's oven or pouring oil on Phyllis's oven mitts — she and her crew might have seen it."

"And did they?"

"Didn't seem like it, but she said she'd let me know if anything came up. She seems trustworthy."

"But what if she isn't?" said Tavi. "What if she went and destroyed the video evidence before anyone could see it? What if *Meg* is actually the saboteur?"

"Whoa." Alice had never considered this.

"Seems unlikely," said Henry. "My powers of intuition tell me that Meg's a really bad liar. But you're right, Tavi, it's a possibility. I'll add her *and* the rest of the camera crew to our list of suspects."

Alice fiddled with her spoon. The more she thought about it, the more it seemed that *anyone* could be the saboteur, from the makeup artists to the cleanup crew to the sound and lighting people.

Even the other contestants.

"Can we trust *anybody*?" she wondered aloud.

"Only each other," said Tavi. "And probably our parents."

"Look, you guys, it's important not to get overwhelmed," Henry told them. "Good detectives try to focus on one thing at a time: one clue, one suspect. Eventually, they piece it all together."

It sounded a bit like baking a charlotte russe, which Alice had no desire to do ever again.

"It's getting busy in here," Tavi noted, glancing around the dining room.

"We should go," Henry said. "You guys up for more detecting?"

"Always," said Tavi, and Alice agreed, though she also wanted to check on her father. "Where to this time?"

"I want to go to the scene of the crime. The Great Hall."

"Good idea." Tavi popped the rest of her scone in her mouth and brushed crumbs off her T-shirt.

Alice hesitated. "Won't it be locked? I bet they don't leave the doors open." Truth be told, she had no desire to return to the scene of the crime. She'd only just escaped it.

"I bet I could pick the lock." Henry pocketed his notebook and stood to go.

Just as Alice was about to protest, she spotted a familiar head of shiny black hair across the dining room. Shiny black hair with perfectly trimmed bangs. She hadn't seen Hana since she'd beaned her with an umbrella. And she didn't want to see her now.

"Let's go," she said, hopping out of her chair and making a beeline for the door. "To the scene of the crime."

When they reached the Great Hall, they found the door not only unlocked, but slightly ajar.

"Guess I won't have to pick the lock." Henry sounded disappointed.

"Can you actually pick locks?" Tavi sounded skeptical.

"Sure," he replied. "I mean, I've only done it at home, but it's not so hard. I have a great app on my phone that teaches you how." He peered through the doorway and looked around. "No one here. Come on."

Alice glanced back down the hallway. She couldn't imagine why the crew would have left the door open, unless they'd just stepped out and planned to return soon. "We have to be careful and quick."

"We'll be both," Henry promised.

"Wow," Tavi said as they tiptoed inside. "This is where you compete? It's incredible."

"Which station was your dad's?" Henry asked. Alice pointed, and he hurried off to inspect it.

Tavi sniffed the air. "Butter and sugar and vanilla. My favorite scent."

It was Alice's too, but she was too nervous to appreciate it. "We should really hurry —"

Tavi held up a hand. "Did you hear that?"

Alice froze and held her breath. There were voices in the hall, growing louder. "Oh *no*."

"Is there another way out?" Tavi looked around.

"I don't think so. Let's hide!"

"Henry!" they whisper-called. "People coming!"

He looked up from the stove he'd been inspecting, then dropped to the floor. Alice and Tavi ran for the farthest workstation, where Sven had been cooking earlier that day. They dove behind it just as the voices entered the hall.

"It's this one over here," someone said. Alice peeked around the station and saw Jasmina marching across the room, followed by Richard Sibley-McFinch and a woman with a toolbox. They stopped in front of James's stove, and Alice held her breath, waiting for the shouting that would mean they'd discovered Henry. But the adults went on discussing the glitchy stove.

Tavi tugged her back. "What happened to Henry?"

"He must have hidden," Alice whispered. "Maybe in a cupboard?"

"A *cupboard*?" Tavi squeaked. Alice shushed her. She'd just heard another set of footsteps enter the hall — or rather pawsteps, skittering across the wood floors.

"Roslyn!" They scooched closer together.

"Ah, there's the problem," said the woman with the tools. "This switch got stuck, so the element was staying hot even when the temperature dial was on low. It happens, although I've never seen it happen to all the elements at once. Still, it's an easy fix."

"So James was telling the truth." Jasmina sounded relieved.

From her hiding place, Alice wanted to shout, "Of *course* he was telling the truth!" It took all her willpower to stay quiet and listen.

"What happens now?" asked Richard. "Roslyn, sweetheart, get away from that! I'm sorry, she's been acting up lately. Ros!"

"Tom Truffleman is holding a meeting tonight to decide whether James is guilty of stealing Samir's saucepan." Jasmina sighed. "He's making a big deal out of nothing, but that's typical Truffleman."

"Manufacturing drama?" Tavi murmured, but before Alice could answer, Roslyn began to bark. Tavi grabbed Alice's arm.

"There, it's fixed! All ready for the next challenge."

"Wish I could say the same for myself," Jasmina grumbled. "I can't wait for this to end." The adults headed for the door.

Alice was just about to relax when Roslyn began to howl.

"Roslyn!" Richard shouted. "Come here! What are you doing?"

"I bet she smells Henry!" Tavi hissed.

Alice peeked around the station again. The whippet was sitting in front of a painting of a sullen old man with a scowl not unlike Tom Truffleman's. She raised her snout and howled again.

"Come on, Rossy, it's dinnertime!" Richard called in a sing-song voice. "I hear there's roast beef on the menu tonight!"

Finally, the dog stood and trotted over to join him at the door. Richard shut it behind them.

"*Another* close call!" Tavi groaned. "That dog is killing me!"

They hurried over to find Henry crawling out of the cupboard next to James's oven. "Did anyone get a good look at that woman who fixed the stove?" he asked, shaking out his legs.

Alice described her as best she could: shoulder-length blond hair, denim overalls. "Another suspect?"

"Maybe," he said.

"No one can be trusted," Tavi said grimly as they sneaked back out of the Great Hall. "Not even that crazy dog. Oh my gosh, imagine if *she* were the saboteur!" She laughed. "Roslyn Sibley-McFinch, canine mastermind!"

Henry snorted, and Alice managed a smile. But her mind was now on the meeting Jasmina had mentioned, where Tom Truffleman would determine her father's fate. She had a bad feeling about it.

She worried about it all evening, even after she and Tavi had turned out the light between their beds. After lying awake for what felt like hours, she pulled out her phone and searched for a distraction. When nothing on PHOMO did the trick, she looked for information about Marie-Antoine Carême's pastry sculptures.

Of course, no photos of his masterpieces existed, but she found some sketches on a food history blog. The crumbling ruins, turreted castles and stately towers made entirely of sugar and butter were even more intricate than she'd imagined. They made her want to try her hand at pastry architecture too.

Eventually, Alice drifted off to sleep, only to dream that her father was trapped in a burning manor made of ladyfinger cookies and that she was the only one who could save him.

CHAPTER

19

T he next day, they staked out a table on the terrace, in the shade of a big white umbrella. From there, they could spy on guests eating lunch, playing croquet on the lawn and hunting for ferns in the trees.

"I think we should add all the contestants to our list of suspects," Henry told them. "Except Alice, obviously."

"And her dad," Tavi added. When Henry hesitated, she gave him a wide-eyed look. "Henry!"

"He's my *dad!*" cried Alice.

"It's just that good detectives don't trust anyone. Sherlock Holmes didn't even —"

"My dad is *not* the saboteur!"

"Okay, okay." Henry scratched something off his list and mumbled, "Sorry."

"Thank you," she huffed. Waiting for Tom Truffleman's verdict was agonizing enough. She didn't need Henry's suspicions on top of that.

"Let's start researching the other contestants." Tavi pulled out her phone. "Look for social media accounts, personal websites, anything you can find. I'll start with Phyllis."

"But Phyllis is gone," Alice pointed out. "She left right after she lost the pigeon pie challenge."

"You never know what you might find on the Internet," said Tavi. "Plus, I want to see more of her wardrobe. I love a good tweed pantsuit."

Alice was fairly certain she wasn't kidding.

"Yeah, look her up," said Henry. "We should investigate everyone, even the contestants who left."

Though Alice couldn't imagine Sven and Samir being behind the sabotage, she Googled their names and quickly came up with the website for their catering company, Saffron Fine Foods. She found menus they'd cooked for weddings and bar mitzvahs and photos of the pair in their matching neckties, but nothing that looked even remotely suspicious.

"Wow," Tavi said after a few minutes. "Phyllis isn't on the Internet at all! She has no website, no PHOMO, no nothing. How is that possible? *Everyone's* on the Internet."

"That's kind of suspicious," said Henry. "But she might just be old-fashioned."

Alice nodded, picturing the blancmange-loving historian. She was probably like her father, who'd only agreed to post a personal page on his university's website because Alice had insisted he needed one. Every year she had to update it for him.

"I found François." Henry held up his phone. Tavi and Alice leaned in to see the latest photo on François's PHOMO account: a selfie he'd taken in front of an hourglass-shaped swimming pool. He was holding a drink decorated with a pineapple wedge, and his nose was pink from sunburn. "Lovin' life in Belize!" read the caption. "This place is incredible!!!"

"Isn't he breaking his contract by posting on PHOMO?" Henry wondered.

Alice wasn't sure, but she was relieved to see François looking happy, after all he'd been through. "I guess we can take him off the —"

"Parents coming!" Tavi hissed suddenly. "Look innocent."

"Huh?" Alice looked up to see Tavi's parents strolling across the terrace toward them. Her father was dressed in pin-striped trousers and a matching vest over a crisp, white shirt. Her mother wore a crimson dress that matched her hair, which was just like Tavi's but streaked with silver.

"Did you tell them about the investigation?" Henry whispered.

"Of course not," Tavi whispered back. "Hi, guys!" she called, a little too loudly.

"Hi, kids," said Mr. Sapphire. "What's up?"

Tavi smiled. "Absolutely nothing. How was your lecture?"

"That sounds suspicious!" Mrs. Sapphire laughed.

Henry kicked Tavi under the table.

"The lecture was excellent," Mr. Sapphire said. "We learned a lot about Victorian politics and social issues — the professor was full of excellent information. Unfortunately, we were practically the only ones there."

"You know how it is sometimes," Mrs. Sapphire said to Tavi.

"How what is?" asked Alice.

"Sometimes people at events like this don't want to experience what life was *really* like back then," Tavi explained. "Because, let's be honest, most of us wouldn't have lived like this." She gestured to the other guests on the terrace. "Most of us would have been working downstairs, cooking and cleaning or whatever."

"This professor reminded us that the Victorian era was also a time of slavery, colonialism and the struggle for women's rights," said Mrs. Sapphire. "She was a little disappointed that so few people showed up to hear about it."

"So we decided to invite her — Oh, there she is now! Hana!" Mr. Sapphire waved across the terrace.

"Hana?" Henry whipped around so fast he nearly fell out of his chair.

"Oh no." Alice's stomach sank. Of course it was Hana.

"Come join us!" Mrs. Sapphire called to Hana. "Henry, have you met Hana already?"

"We've all met Hana," Tavi said, giving Alice a sympathetic look.

Hana started at the sight of Alice fidgeting in her chair, and Alice winced at the plum-colored bruise around Hana's right eye.

"We had no idea you knew all the kids already," said Mrs. Sapphire. "We were just telling them about your excellent lecture."

"That's kind of you." Hana smiled. Then she turned to Alice. "I hear you cooked by yourself yesterday, Alice. And that you did an amazing job."

"Me? Oh, um, yes. I mean, sort of. I mean, thanks." Alice mumbled. Henry gave her a funny look, which she ignored.

"Well, I think that was really brave of you," Hana said quietly.

Alice shrugged, wishing she wouldn't be so nice.

"We're going to go to the spa down the road for a swim," said Mr. Sapphire. "Richard tells us we can get in at a discounted rate for neighbors. And . . ." — he wiggled his eyebrows — "we'll get to show off our Victorian bathing costumes!"

"Dad, no!" Tavi covered her face.

"What's the big deal?" Mrs. Sapphire asked innocently. "We

would have been hot stuff in the 1800s." She winked at Alice and Henry.

"MOM!" Tavi cried, but she was laughing. "Have you guys ever seen a Victorian bathing costume?" she asked Alice and Henry.

Alice nodded — she'd seen photos of women in knee-length dresses over billowy bloomers trimmed with ribbons, and men in striped sleeveless tops and short trousers.

Henry shook his head, looking frightened.

"You should come, Henry!" Mr. Sapphire nudged him. "We can find an authentic suit for you too!"

"Dad! Leave Henry alone," Tavi scolded. "We're staying here."

Mr. Sapphire shrugged. "Hana? Will you come?"

"I think I will," said Hana. "I don't have a Victorian bathing suit, though."

"It's better that way," Tavi assured her. "You can just pretend you don't know my parents."

Hana laughed. Then her smile faded. "Oh, but I want to be around when James finds out . . ." She looked at Alice. "Do you know when that'll be?"

Alice shook her head. She hadn't heard from her father all morning.

"You mean the cooking challenge you told us about?" Mrs. Sapphire asked.

Hana nodded miserably. "It's absolutely ridiculous. I feel terrible for him."

Alice had never seen her look so sad. And she could understand why: the festival hadn't exactly gone as planned for her. First, she'd gotten a black eye. Then she'd lectured to a nearly empty room. And now James was in danger of getting kicked off the show she'd signed him up for, thinking it would be "good exposure."

Serves her right, thought Alice. But she knew that wasn't true. Hana didn't deserve to feel so bad.

"Maybe you need a change of scenery," Mr. Sapphire suggested. "We won't be gone long."

"But we should leave soon," said Mrs. Sapphire. "These petticoats are killing me. Do you have any idea how many layers of underwear Victorian women had to wear?" she asked Alice and Henry. "That's one of the main reasons I wouldn't want to live in this era."

Henry reddened and squirmed.

"Go! Swim!" Tavi shooed her parents away. "And please, *please* don't post any photos."

"All right, enjoy the afternoon," said Mr. Sapphire. "Don't spend it all on your phones."

"We won't!" Tavi waved goodbye.

As soon as the adults had left, they pulled out their phones and got back to work.

By mid-afternoon, the terrace was sweltering hot, even in the shade, and they still hadn't found any promising clues. They decided to continue their investigation indoors.

But they'd just stepped into the lobby when Alice saw her father. He was sitting on a sofa near the fireplace, staring into space. She hurried over, and Henry and Tavi followed.

"What's wrong?" she demanded, plopping down beside him. "What did they say?"

He heaved a sigh, then reported that he'd been deemed

guilty of theft on *Culinary Combat*. Jasmina had just told him. He was out of the competition.

"No!" Alice grabbed his arm.

"You've got to be kidding!" cried Tavi.

James tugged at his hair. "I'm so sorry, Alice. What a stupid thing to happen."

"We'll protest!" she assured him. "We'll make them change their minds."

"We're very persuasive," added Tavi.

He gave her a half-smile. "Sadly, I've already tried that. This is their final decision."

"But it's not fair! You didn't do anything wrong." Alice grabbed a cushion and crushed it to her chest. "They found a problem with your stove, didn't they?"

He blinked at her. "How did you know that?"

"We heard a rumor," Henry said quickly.

James sighed. "Well, that's true. They did find a problem with the stove. But the fact remains that I stole Samir's saucepan, even if it was just an accident. They're calling it the great strawberry scandal of Season 1. How stupid." He rubbed his temples. "And to think all this will be on TV."

They all fell silent, imagining it.

"So what happens now?" Alice asked eventually. "Do we have to go home?"

"Now?" Tavi gasped. "You can't leave now!"

"Well, here's the thing," said James. "The competition will go on as planned tomorrow, and you're still in it, Alice. If you want to be."

Alice stared at him. "I am?"

He nodded. "You'd have to compete alone against the two other teams, and I'm told it's going to be a long challenge.

According to Jasmina, there will be two parts: one in the morning and one in the afternoon."

"Alone," she repeated. It hadn't occurred to her that she'd have to cook by herself again.

"You don't have to," he assured her. "No one would blame you if you said no."

She hugged the sofa cushion and tried to picture herself refusing to cook. They could pack up their things, head home and try to forget everything that had happened.

It was definitely tempting.

But one look at her friends told her she couldn't leave now. They still had a saboteur to catch. And now she had her father's name to clear.

Which left her only one option, and it wasn't going to be fun.

"I guess . . . I'll do it?" she said quietly. Henry nodded. Tavi squeezed her arm.

"Really?" James looked shocked. "I mean, of course you're capable of it. But . . . do you really want to, Alice?"

She could think of few things she wanted to do less. But that wasn't the point.

"When does the challenge start?"

"Nine o'clock, apparently," said James. "I guess they're letting the competitors sleep in a bit. Maybe they plan to go easy on you." They both laughed at that. "Look, why don't you think about it some more," he suggested, standing up. "We can talk about it later. In the meantime, I'm going to go find Hana and let her know what happened."

"She might still be at the spa with my parents," Tavi told him.

"Ah. Well." He nodded absently, then wandered off across the lobby.

"Your poor dad," Tavi said, watching him go. "And poor you too," she added.

Alice swallowed hard. "I can't believe I have to cook by myself. Again."

"You won't be by yourself," said Henry.

She sighed. "I *know* there'll be other people around, but that's not the point. They can't help me."

"I meant that we'll be there with you."

"You will?" She looked at him.

"We will?" said Tavi.

He nodded. "We have to be. It's our last chance to catch the saboteur in action."

"But . . . how?" asked Tavi. "We're not allowed in there."

"The competition starts at nine o'clock, so let's sneak in around seven and find a good hiding place. Those cupboards aren't so bad."

"I'm half a foot taller than you," Tavi pointed out. "I can't fit in a cupboard."

"We'll find someplace else, then," said Henry. "The point is, we'll do the detecting while Alice concentrates on cooking. Okay?"

"Okay," Tavi said, though she clearly wasn't sure about the plan.

Alice wasn't either, but it made her feel better to know that her friends would be with her. She had a feeling she'd need all the support she could get to survive the final challenge . . . which, knowing Tom Truffleman, would surely be the worst!

CHAPTER

20

A lice felt as though she'd only just fallen asleep that night when a knock on the door woke her.

She sat bolt upright, wondering if it was already morning, if she'd slept past her alarm. But the sky outside her window was still dark, and when she checked her phone, it read 4:45 a.m.

She'd just decided that she must have dreamed the knocking when it happened again: three short raps. In the bed beside hers, Tavi mumbled in her sleep.

Alice tossed the covers aside. If someone was knocking at 4:45 a.m., it had to be an emergency. She hurried to the door and swung it open, expecting to see her father, or maybe the Sapphires.

Instead, she found Jasmina.

"Huh?" Alice blinked hard, wondering once again if she was dreaming.

The producer gave her an apologetic smile. "I'm so sorry, Alice. But there's been a change in plans."

And that was how Alice knew she was very much awake. *Of course* there had been a change in plans.

"This morning's challenge begins at five o'clock. In fifteen minutes." Jasmina's eyes were wide, as if she couldn't believe it herself.

Alice gaped.

"Again, I'm so sorry. If it helps, there's coffee downstairs in the lobby."

Alice began to say that, as a twelve-year-old, she didn't drink much coffee, but Jasmina waved her back inside to get dressed. She did as she was told and shut the door. "I can't believe it," she said. Though of course she could. This made all the sense in the world.

"Believe what?" Tavi murmured. "And why are you up in the middle of the night?"

"It's 4:45," Alice told her. "And they changed the rules again. I have to cook now." Her voice broke on the last word.

"What? No. Am I dreaming?" Tavi rolled over and flicked on the bedside lamp.

"I wish." Alice quickly changed from her pajamas to the jeans and T-shirt she'd worn the day before. She didn't care that they were dirty.

"Wait, but our plan!" Tavi sat up. "Henry's still asleep — we weren't going to sneak in until seven!" She threw her covers off. "I'll go wake him up."

"I think it's too late," Alice said as she braided her hair. "The Great Hall will already be packed with people."

Tavi groaned. "I hate Tom Truffleman!"

"Me too." Alice finished her braid and tossed it over her shoulder. "I have to go."

"I'll wake Henry anyway. We'll make a new plan."

Alice let herself out of the room, too full of feelings to answer. She stayed quiet as she followed Jasmina down the stairs to the lobby, where the other contestants were waiting.

Tina was yawning, Toni glowering. Samir was downing a big mug of coffee. Only Sven looked bright-eyed and relaxed.

"Sven is a morning person," Samir grumbled when Alice and Jasmina joined them. "I've never understood it."

Sven shrugged. "It's a great time to be awake." Samir shook his head and took another swig of coffee.

"Alice?"

She turned to see Hana on the staircase.

"What's going on?" Hana hurried down the stairs and over to the contestants. "You're not about to start cooking, are you?"

"Uh-huh." Alice glanced at her jogging pants and sneakers. "Are you going for a run? Now?"

Hana nodded. "It's my favorite time of day."

"See?" said Sven.

"That's insane," Samir grumped.

Hana ignored them and turned back to Alice. "Your dad doesn't know, does he? He's going to be so upset! He planned to be down here at seven-thirty so he wouldn't miss you. Should I go wake him?"

"We have to get started," Jasmina told her. "Everyone needs more time for makeup today."

"Wait, have you eaten?" Hana asked. When Alice shook her head, she pulled a granola bar out of her pocket. "Take this. I'll tell your dad what happened."

"Thank you." Alice took the granola bar, heartened by the fact that it was covered in chocolate.

"Oh, Alice, I'm —"

"We're going in!" called Jasmina.

"I have to go," said Alice. "I'll be okay," she added, because Hana looked positively ill. Then she turned and followed the others to the Great Hall, where three workstations awaited them. Alice would be cooking at the middle station, behind Samir and Sven and in front of the twins. None of the others were paying any attention to her now, though they were usually so kind and supportive. Everyone was too caught up in their own worries — or maybe just too tired. Either way, it made her feel very alone.

She settled into her station, desperately wishing Tavi and Henry were there. For a moment, she allowed herself to pretend that everything had gone according to plan, and they were close by, maybe hiding in a cupboard. She felt her whole body relax.

And then she noticed Tom Truffleman. He was off in a corner, talking to Jasmina and Miranda. The producer's face looked stormy, the host's incredulous. But Tom Truffleman looked perfectly content, even peaceful — as though he'd had a very good night's sleep on a very fluffy pillow.

What did he have planned for them? Alice's whole body tightened again. It would be a difficult challenge, no doubt about it. Maybe even impossible.

Once the sound crew had attached the contestants' microphones and the makeup crew had covered the bags under their eyes, Miranda took her place at the front of the room and faced the cameras.

"Ready?" Jasmina called.

Miranda swallowed, smoothed her ponytail and nodded. Soon the cameras were rolling, and the host explained the day's challenge.

"This is not only the last day of our competition, it's also the last day of the festival here at Gladstone Manor," Miranda said. "Tonight, there will be a feast for the guests, and you," she turned to the contestants, "will prepare it. That's why you're here so ridiculously early," she added apologetically. "It's going to take a while."

Alice gasped. An entire *feast*?

"In your drawer, you'll find the menu, with recipes. Some of the instructions will be clear, and sometimes you'll have to be creative. You've got five hours this morning to prepare whichever dishes you think you should make first — that's up to you. Then we'll take a break before cooking for another five hours. The feast begins at seven o'clock," Miranda finished. "Okay?"

The competitors gaped at her.

"So you should, like, probably get started."

They all fumbled for their menus and recipes. In the top drawer of her station, Alice found a stack of papers topped with a menu titled "A Victorian Feast." Hands trembling, she set the papers on the countertop and began to read.

A Victorian Feast

—

Five loaves of bread
Soup for twenty guests
Three vegetable dishes of your choice
One swan pie
One traditional jelly dessert to serve twenty guests

For a moment, the entire hall was very quiet. Then Toni shouted, "*Swan pie? You want us to cook a swan?*"

"No!" Alice dropped her menu.

"Well." Miranda cast a desperate look around the room. "Actually . . ."

"That's exactly what we wanted you to do," Tom Truffleman declared, marching to the front of the set with his hands on his

192

hips. "It wasn't a common dish in that era, but swan can be very tasty. Especially the young ones — like pigeons, swans are only worth eating when they're young."

"That is disgusting!" cried Toni.

"However," the judge went on, "although we tried very hard, we weren't able to procure any swans for this challenge. So instead we chose the next best thing."

"Chicken?" Samir said hopefully. "Please say it's chicken."

Tom Truffleman smiled wolfishly. "Better than chicken. For tonight's feast, you'll be making . . . a peacock pie."

"Peacock!" Toni exploded.

"No!" Alice cried. Peacock pie? Again? And *on* TV?! "But that's not a Victorian dish! It's from the Middle Ages — that's centuries earlier!"

Possibly he didn't hear her, but more likely he didn't care. "That is your challenge," he said smugly. "Make me a feast I'll never forget. Or lose." He shrugged, then walked off set.

"Wait, look at this!" Samir said, flipping through his papers. "The dessert recipe calls for gelatin, but it's not on our list of available ingredients. Does that mean we have to make it ourselves?"

"*No.*" Alice flipped through her papers, praying he was wrong. He wasn't.

"We can do that," Sven assured him.

"Do you know what that entails?" Samir sputtered.

"This menu is enormous!" Toni wailed. "How are we going to make it all? Also, who in their right mind would want to cook a peacock?"

"I think they're using us as free labor!" Samir declared. "I know the hotel is short-staffed, but this is ridiculous."

"Let's just get started," said Sven.

"I don't know where to start," Samir retorted.

Toni threw her hands in the air. "We've never done anything like this!"

I have, thought Alice. She'd made every one of the dishes on the menu. And that was precisely the problem: she knew just how awful it would be to make a jelly dessert from scratch and bake a peacock pie. It was as if Tom Truffleman had purposely chosen the dishes she found most torturous.

Could that be true? she wondered. He must have seen the video of her making peacock pie with her father. And she had mentioned, during the second challenge, that she wasn't a fan of making gelatin.

Maybe he actually *was* trying to torture her! She couldn't say for sure. But if that was his plan, it wasn't going to work. She would not let Tom Truffleman win.

While the other contestants bickered, Alice quietly got to work. And since she knew it would take a very long time, she began to make her gelatin.

In one of the fridges, she found three long, thin objects wrapped in parchment paper and labeled "Calf's Foot." She allowed herself a moment for a full-body shudder, then grabbed one of the packages and brought it back to her station, where she filled a pot of water and set it on the stove to boil. She knew without even looking at the recipe that the foot would need to simmer in the water for a few hours, at which point she'd take it out, strain the liquid, then set it aside for several more hours until it congealed into a jelly-like substance. Then she'd add flavoring to make it into a dessert.

She would not, she was certain, be eating that dessert.

Drawing a deep breath, she unwrapped the offending foot, dropped it in her pot and covered it quickly. Only then did she notice the video camera beside her, filming her every move.

There she was, boiling a calf's foot for the entire world to see. And not on the History Alive network, but on RealiTV. Her worst nightmare had actually, finally come true. It made her knees wobble, and she clutched the counter to keep herself from falling.

"Here." Miranda appeared at her side with another glass of water. "You look pale. Are you okay?" Before Alice could answer, Miranda turned to the videographer. "You get out of here. Go!" She shooed him away, then turned back to Alice. "Drink up."

Alice did as she was told, noting that the host looked rather pale herself. "Are *you* okay?"

Miranda lowered her voice. "Honestly, I find this so stressful. The tension, the smell, the ... the feet." She waved at the pot on Alice's stove, as if trying to shoo that away too.

"Everyone's stressed," Alice said, taking another sip of water. And it was only the beginning of a ten-hour challenge.

"We all need to calm down," Miranda agreed. Then she gasped. "I know! Can you tell a story?"

"Sorry, what?" Alice swallowed.

"You know, like James does. Everyone loves his stories. They're so calming."

Alice looked down at the stack of recipes awaiting her, then back up at the host. "I don't know ..."

"But you could try?"

Alice wondered if this was how parents felt when their children begged for bedtime stories. Except she was the child, and Miranda was the adult.

Adults are so weird, she thought. Then she sighed. "Okay. I'll try."

"Great! Hey, be quiet," Miranda said, shushing the cleaning crew nearby. She signaled to the videographer she'd just turned away. "You, come back." Then she looked at Alice expectantly. "Whenever you're ready."

"Give me a minute," Alice said. Her father always knew which story to tell — he had one for every dish they made. She looked at the feast menu, thinking hard. "Okay," she said. "Here's one about peacock pie."

"Ew, really?" Miranda made a face. "How about something —"

"Who's telling the story here?" Alice asked, exasperated.

"Sorry, sorry." Miranda motioned for her to proceed.

"So, peacocks are originally from India," Alice began, as her father had a few months before. "And all throughout history, people have known they were special. Some people saw them as a symbol of wealth. To others, they represented immortality."

This, she believed, was an excellent reason not to eat them, but she kept that to herself.

"In medieval Europe, peacock was a special treat served at the fanciest banquets. It sounds awful, but people would skin the peacock, cook it, then dress it back up in its feathers before serving it."

Miranda looked as though she was regretting asking for a story.

"But this pie is special not just because of the peacock, but because of the spices in it. Did you know that only the richest Europeans had access to spices in the Middle Ages? The spices came from Asia and North Africa — places most Europeans would never visit in their lives. Spices were a status symbol: the more you had, the more important you were. They were like sports cars today, or expensive clothes or . . ."

"Handbags?" Miranda offered. "Or maybe a really good moisturizer."

"Sure," said Alice. "Anyway, the people who sold the spices — they were called spice merchants — they knew that these rich nobles wanted spices very badly, so they decided to raise the prices. And then they made up crazy stories about how hard it was to get the spices so the buyers would believe they were worth all the money. Some told stories of a mythical bird called the cinnamologus, whose nests were made of cinnamon sticks and perched on steep cliffsides. They said that to harvest the cinnamon they'd had to climb the cliffs and lure the cinnamologus birds away from their nests."

"No!" Miranda sipped from the water glass she'd brought for Alice.

Alice nodded. "And they got away with it, because the people buying the spices weren't about to travel across the world to see for themselves."

"Wow," said Miranda.

"I heard that story for the first time a few months ago," Alice went on, feeling comfortable enough now to talk a bit about herself. "My dad decided we had to make a peacock pie for dinner, just like this. But he forgot to tell me his new girlfriend was coming over. I met her for the first time while I was stuffing peacock into a pie."

Miranda grimaced.

"It gets worse," Alice told her. "He forgot that she's vegetarian."

Behind her, the twins chuckled. Even the videographer was smiling.

"Oh no, what did she do?" asked Miranda.

Alice recalled how Hana had pulled up a chair at the kitchen table to watch. She'd asked questions about peacocks and spice merchants and shared some of her own knowledge too. Alice had learned that in Roman times some soldiers were paid in salt, since it was so valuable. The word *salary* actually came from "salt," as did the word *salad*, since the Romans used salt to flavor their vegetables.

Later, Hana had helped her make a salad so there would be something other than peacock to eat.

"She just kind of went with it," said Alice. "She's actually pretty cool that way."

"She sounds like a gem," said Miranda.

Alice considered this. "Well, maybe —"

"Competitors!" Tom Truffleman hollered, making everyone jump. "Nearly one hour has now passed. If you're not hard at work, you're going to be in big trouble!"

Miranda winked at Alice. "I'll let you get back to work," she said. "Thanks for the story."

"Yes, thank you, Alice." Samir turned to give her a smile.

"It was exactly what we needed," said Tina.

Alice grinned. Feeling surprisingly refreshed, she turned back to her menu.

Next, she decided, she would bake her bread, since it would need time to rise. The recipe instructions were rather vague, but she knew how to make bread. She gathered her ingredients, then prepared a large batch of dough and kneaded it until it was smooth and elastic. Then she put her dough in a bowl, covered it and tucked it into the warming drawer at the bottom of her oven, where she left it to rise for an hour.

With that task complete, she had no choice but to face the peacock. The recipe was similar to the one she and her father had followed, but Alice decided she would use fewer spices this time and marinate the meat in them for several hours so the pie would be flavorful but not spicy enough to make the guests' eyes water.

She found a box in the fridge with her name on it and hauled it back to her workstation, praying, as she had when the peacock arrived in a box on their doorstep, that it would be plucked.

"Thank you thank you thank you," she whispered on seeing that it was. She lifted it out of the box and, just as she'd seen her father do, began to cut it up for the pie.

"You are incredible, Alice," Meg said as she passed by. "No matter how this competition ends, you're going to be a star. A twelve-year-old kid cooking peacock pie by herself? Like it's no big deal?" She laughed. "That's gold."

Alice wasn't sure what to say to that, so she gave Meg a thumbs-up, then went back to work.

CHAPTER 21

F ive hours, one pot of vegetable soup, five loaves of bread and one pie's worth of prepared peacock later, Alice emerged from the Great Hall. Her braid was unraveled, her face flushed and her arms smeared with things she didn't want to think about. She felt equal parts satisfied and completely exhausted.

Jasmina led them to the parlor, where they would have an hour to eat lunch and rest before returning to cook for another five hours. Alice had hoped to see her father as they crossed the lobby, but he wasn't there. Not that it mattered, anyway — they'd been instructed not to speak to anyone except each other over the break.

As soon as they reached the parlor, Sven and Samir collapsed on one of the sofas. Alice claimed an armchair across from them.

"The serving staff will bring you coffee, tea and sandwiches," Jasmina promised. "I'll let them know you're ready. In the meantime, get some rest."

"Done." Samir covered his eyes with his arm and promptly went to sleep. Sven kicked off his shoes and closed his eyes. Toni and Tina, meanwhile, moved to the window seat across the room, where they sat with their heads close together, whispering. Watching them made Alice envious — after cooking alone for five hours, she longed for someone to talk to.

"Sandwich?"

"Oh, thanks," Alice said to the server who'd appeared beside her. She was reaching for what looked like egg salad when she noticed that Tavi was holding the tray. "Oh my gosh!"

Tavi grinned. "Great outfit, huh?" She was wearing a Victorian housemaid's costume: a long, black dress covered with a white apron. "Check out Henry!"

Alice gasped as Henry tottered through the door carrying a tea service and wearing a black suit. "You guys!" she squealed, then clapped a hand over her mouth. But Samir and Sven were still napping, Toni and Tina still chatting on the window seat — no one seemed to have noticed.

"How did you get here?" Alice whispered as Tavi set the sandwiches down and crouched beside her.

"We started by raiding the costume room," Tavi began. "Henry wasn't into it at first, but I think he secretly loves his outfit. Right, Henry?"

Henry sniffed. "It's called working undercover."

"Then we convinced Richard to let us help the serving staff. We told him we wanted an authentic experience, because if we'd actually lived in Victorian times, most of us would have had lower-class jobs. I don't think he'd ever thought of that before." She shrugged. "Anyway, the staff was happy to let us help out. They're busy setting up for this big feast tonight."

"How's the challenge going?" Henry asked as he poured tea into a dainty cup for Alice. "The tuna's really good, by the way."

She took a tuna sandwich and gave them a hasty report of the morning's events.

"An entire feast?" Tavi shook her head and helped herself to a tuna sandwich as well. "That's bananas!"

"I guess you haven't had any time to watch for the saboteur," said Henry.

Alice shook her head — she'd barely even thought about it. "I haven't seen anything suspicious, but we still have five hours to go."

"How's everyone doing?" Jasmina asked, marching back into the room.

Tavi shoved the rest of her sandwich into her mouth.

"Gotta go." Henry picked up the tea service. "Jeez, this thing's heavy."

"You've got this, Alice," Tavi whispered over a mouthful of tuna. "We believe in you!"

"Good luck," Henry added as he shuffled off with the tea.

Alice smiled as she watched her friends circle the parlor in their serving costumes. She was still smiling when the lunch break ended and Jasmina led them back to the Great Hall.

You've got this, she repeated to herself as she went to the fridge to collect her pie filling. Maybe Tavi was right. She still had to cook three vegetable dishes, along with a pie and a dessert, but as long as nothing disastrous happened, it just might be possible. Her heart thrilled a little at the thought.

But when she saw her dish of pie filling, her heart sank again. The meat was covered not only with spices but with what looked like . . . She peered more closely.

Slime.

"Oh no," she breathed. "*Oh no.*" She closed her eyes and opened them, but it was still there: a thin layer of green slime, all over the meat.

"Ready to start, Alice?" Jasmina called. "We're rolling in three minutes!"

"Not exactly." She sank to her knees in front of the fridge, cradling the dish.

"What on earth!?"

She looked up to see Tom Truffleman whipping off his glasses. "What happened?"

"I don't know," she whispered. "But it doesn't look good."

"It looks horrendous!" he agreed. "Did it spoil? Did you leave the fridge door open?"

She didn't think so — after all, everything else in the fridge looked fine. And anyway, she'd only been gone an hour, not long enough for slime to grow.

"Well, you can't feed people spoiled meat," he pointed out unhelpfully. Then he walked away.

She groaned.

"Alice? We're about to start!"

"I don't know what to do," she whispered to the meat. It glistened like green Jell-o.

Come to think of it, it *did* look a lot like green Jell-o. She leaned closer, and a thought popped into her head. What if the saboteur had smeared Jell-o on her dish to make it look as if it had spoiled? Was that even possible?

She sniffed the dish. Was that . . . a hint of lime? She wasn't sure, and she definitely wasn't going to taste it. She longed to to talk to Tavi and Henry: was this another case of sabotage? But even if it was, what was she going to do? Her dish was ruined — she couldn't feed it to the guests.

She put it back in the fridge and slumped back to her workstation.

"Rolling!" Meg cried, and everyone leapt into action, picking up where they'd left off.

Everyone except Alice. She stood at her station, hands in her apron pockets, wanting at once to cry, to hide, and to find the saboteur and whack them with an umbrella.

"Alice?" Miranda hurried over. "Why aren't you working? You've only got five more hours to finish — Oh." She stopped when Alice began to sniffle. Then she dashed off and returned with another glass of water and a tissue. "What's going on?"

Alice blew her nose, gulped down some water and explained her predicament.

"Slime!" Miranda looked horrified. "See, this is why I don't cook! I'd spoil meat for sure."

Alice wanted to point out that she hadn't spoiled the meat herself. At least, she didn't think she had.

She blew her nose again.

"It's going to be okay," Miranda assured her. "So . . . what do you think you'll do?"

"I don't know." She looked around at the other competitors, who were busy assembling their pies. She took another sip of water and tried to think.

"I guess . . . I can still make a few things," she said eventually. "My bread is done, and it turned out fine. So did the soup."

"Good," Miranda said encouragingly. "That's something."

She nodded. "I can still make the vegetable dishes. Those are actually pretty important — a lot of Victorians were vegetarian, you know."

"I'll leave you to it, then," said Miranda. "You'll be okay?"

"I'll be okay," said Alice. And it was true. She wasn't going to win the competition — there was no hope of that now. But she did have several hours to cook some nice vegetarian dishes and a dessert.

And maybe the dessert could be something special . . .

She set her glass down with a thunk, making Miranda jump. "I've got it."

"Got what?"

"A new plan." Alice marched back to the fridge and returned minutes later with carrots, beets, potatoes, eggplant and tomatoes. Those vegetarians were going to feast.

She was just peeling the potatoes when Tina cleared her throat. "Did I ever tell you guys about our abuelita's churros?"

Alice glanced back, unsure who she was talking to.

"Growing up, we lived in Mexico City," Tina went on. "But on weekends, we'd drive out to the countryside to visit our abuelita, our grandmother. And she made the very best churros in the world. Have you guys ever had churros?"

Alice nodded. She and James sometimes bought the sticks of fried pastry dough dusted in cinnamon sugar from a street vendor near the university. They always devoured them on the spot.

"I've tried a lot of churros in my life," said Toni. "And I can say with all certainty that our abuelita made the very best."

"She also couldn't tell us apart," added Tina.

"Nope!" Toni laughed. "And we took advantage of that! Every time we went to visit, we'd dress identically, right down to our socks. When she started serving the churros, we'd make sure to split up. Then later I'd come back for seconds, and when she'd tell me I'd already had my share, I'd insist that it was Tina, not me. Then Tina would come later and do the same. It was a great game."

They laughed together, and Alice smiled, imagining the twins as sneaky children. She saw more smiles around the room, though Tom Truffleman was frowning, as usual.

She'd just turned back to her potatoes when Samir spoke up. "As long as we're talking about our favorite foods," he said, "have I told you guys about my minor addiction to tahini?"

"Minor!" Sven snorted. "You go through a jar every week!"

"And I've really cut back," Samir insisted. "Tahini is one of the greatest foods in the world. Has everyone tried it?"

Alice had. "It's like a sesame paste. We eat it in hummus."

"Exactly," said Samir. "It's also the main ingredient in . . ." He paused dramatically. "Halva."

"Oh, here we go," said Sven.

"What's that?" Miranda asked.

"Halva is a Middle Eastern delicacy," said Samir. "It's kind of like fudge, but it's made with tahini and sweetened with honey. I learned to make it from my mother, who always said that it was easy to make halva, but hard to make it delicious. Because," he paused again, "there's a secret ingredient."

Alice listened closely, taking mental notes for when she'd try to make halva at home.

"Love!" he proclaimed. "If you love the people you're making it for, it will turn out much tastier. If you don't add love, well, it's only so-so."

Sven laughed and shook his head.

"You laugh now," Samir said to him. He turned to the others. "But I made it for Sven when we first met, and look at us now."

Sven reddened, but admitted this to be true.

"Oh my gosh, you guys!" Miranda clapped her hands. "That is *adorable!*"

Now everyone in the hall had stopped to listen, and Tom Truffleman was clearly upset. Alice saw him mouth "What's going on?" to Jasmina, who smiled and shrugged.

"Your turn," Samir said to Sven. "If you don't want to talk about love, you can tell us how you knew you wanted to be a chef."

Sven wiped his hands on his apron. "All right. It was all because of my uncle, who had one of the best jobs in Sweden — at least, I thought so. He made the legendary desserts for the Nobel Prize winners at their annual dinner."

"That's a *job*?" cried Toni.

Sven nodded. "Each year, Nobel Prize winners from all over the world travel to Sweden for a big celebration with a delicious meal. Dessert is always the highlight: for decades, they served a fancy frozen bombe, a dome of cake filled with layers of ice cream and sorbet, decorated with spun sugar and a big N, for Nobel."

"Wow!" Alice took more mental notes.

"When I was a teenager, I became my uncle's assistant and helped prepare these beautiful desserts for some of the most brilliant minds in the world. I even got to serve them in the traditional pyrotechnic parade, with sparklers on every plate. So, I suppose you could say my career started off with a bang."

"Amazing!" Tina and Toni cheered.

Now Tom Truffleman was furious. "They're not even paying attention anymore!" he raged at Jasmina. "This isn't *Culinary Combat!*"

"I'd say it's more like *Culinary Chronicles.*" Toni grinned. "And we have Alice and James to thank for inspiring us."

Alice thought her heart might burst. She felt as light as puff pastry and as bright as a sparkler.

She suddenly felt like cooking.

For the next three and a half hours, she cooked with abandon. She forgot about video cameras, microphones, fierce judges, even the other competitors. At one point, she forgot about the competition altogether.

She whipped up three Victorian vegetable dishes: duchess potatoes, stuffed eggplant, carrots sliced in the shape of stars and cooked in a dill sauce. Then she turned her attention to dessert. By that point, she could picture it perfectly. This would be no boring jelly dessert — in fact, she'd forgotten all about the gelatin she'd made. Her dessert would be something special, a tribute to the Victorians, but in a style all her own.

She began by baking a big chocolate cake. Once it had cooled, she carved it up and arranged the pieces, gluing them together with thick, white icing. Next, she found some fondant and black food coloring paste on the baking supply shelf and kneaded the paste into the fondant to turn it black. Then she rolled out the fondant and draped it over her sculpture, creating a smooth surface for decorating. She brushed on egg whites to make it shiny, then used a tiny paintbrush to add the intricate details.

When it was all finished, she stood back to survey her creation. At first glance, it looked like an old-fashioned telephone with a rotary dial. But when the judge sliced into it, he'd find layers of delicious chocolate cake.

It was a Victorian invention, an object that had changed people's lives. It was also a reminder that inside everything — and everyone — was something unexpected.

It was the best thing she'd ever made.

"Time's up, everyone!" Miranda announced. "That's your final challenge. Leave your dishes on your stations — this time,

Tom will judge them after you've left. We'll announce the winner at the feast, which starts at seven o'clock."

The competitors exhaled collectively and stepped away from their stations, which were piled high with pies and breads, vegetables and jelly desserts and — to everyone's surprise — one old-fashioned telephone.

"Wow, you really went rogue," Meg chuckled to Alice. "Can I get a shot of you standing next to that?"

Alice paused for just a moment before straightening her apron. "You bet," she said, turning toward the camera. And although she knew her hair was flying every which way and she probably had chocolate smeared on her face, she couldn't stop smiling.

CHAPTER 22

When it was all over and Alice stumbled out of the Great Hall for the last time, she found her father in the lobby, reading near the fireplace.

She collapsed on the sofa beside him, and he yelped and dropped his book. "Alice! My god, you scared me. I was totally absorbed in this history of the potato ricer, and —" He shook his head. "Sorry. How did it go? Tell me everything."

She recounted the events of the day, leaving out the part about the spoiled meat, since that was a longer story for another time. He was horrified by the menu, thrilled at how she'd gamely made gelatin while everyone else argued, delighted by her telling of the spice merchant story, elated that she'd sculpted a Victorian telephone and devastated that he hadn't been there to witness it in person.

Her father was a very good audience.

"But . . . but a peacock!" he sputtered once she was finished. "That's not even historically accurate!"

"That's what I said."

He shook his head. "You are absolutely incredible. Have I told you how proud I am? So very proud."

"Thanks." She leaned back and closed her eyes. She knew she had to find Tavi and Henry and tell them about the latest incident of sabotage. But she was just so tired.

"You must be starving," said James. "Let's get you something to eat."

She considered this and discovered he was right.

"But I can't eat pie," she warned him. "Or any kind of bird — not even chicken. And definitely nothing made with gelatin. I'll probably never eat gelatin again."

He nodded. "Let's see what the kitchen can do."

Ten minutes later they were sitting on the terrace, and Alice was working her way through a giant slice of chocolate cake while downing glass after glass of lemonade. It was all the kitchen staff could offer, since they were busy preparing for the feast.

"Normally I'd insist you also eat something healthy," James said, eyeing the cake, "but in this case, I'd say you deserve to eat whatever you want."

Alice agreed. She'd had no idea how much she wanted sweet chocolate frosting and cold, sour lemonade.

As she ate, she described how the other contestants had told stories of the foods they loved and the people who made them, and how Tom Truffleman nearly lost his mind. James laughed so hard he choked on his lemonade.

"I was so upset this morning when I found out how early you started cooking," he told her. "I can't believe they didn't tell me! And I would never even have known if Hana hadn't got up so god-awfully early. She was pretty distraught when she told me, you know. I think she feels guilty for bringing us here in the first place."

Alice took a bite of cake and chewed it for a long time. "It wasn't her fault," she said eventually. "Well, not all of it. I mean, she couldn't have known what was going to happen."

"None of us could have." He stared out at the trees for a while, then turned back to Alice. "While we're on the topic of Hana . . ."

Here we go again, she thought. But she let him go on.

"We have a great life, you and I," he said. "Not a fancy life — nothing like this."

"I don't want this," she told him.

"Me neither." He smiled.

"But . . ." she prompted, steeling herself.

"*And,*" he said carefully, "wouldn't it be nice to have someone else to share it with? Not any time soon, of course. But maybe . . . eventually?"

"Could that be a dog?" she asked, drawing squiggles in her frosting with her fork.

"Alice."

"Dad." She looked up from her cake. "I don't need a mom, if that's what you're thinking."

"That's not what I'm thinking," he assured her. "But I do think it would be nice for you to have another adult around as you're growing up."

She wasn't sure about this, so she turned back to her cake.

"But mostly," he went on, "well, it's human nature to want to love. It's what we do. We connect with people, sometimes deeply. And we want them in our lives."

She set down her fork. "But Dad, aren't you scared? I mean, the love thing didn't exactly work out for you last time."

"Work out for me!" He laughed. "Alice, I got you! That worked out swimmingly."

She allowed this. "But that's not what I mean. What if . . . I don't know. What if she decides she doesn't like us? I mean, you eat meat, and she's vegetarian. She gets up god-awfully early, and you've never even seen a sunrise."

"I've seen a sunrise!" he protested. "Once or twice. A long time ago. Anyway, I know what you mean. It's risky business, opening your heart. And your kitchen. You have to be very brave."

There it was again, that word. It was everywhere these days.

"Are we brave enough?" she wondered to her cake.

"A year or two ago, I would have asked the same thing," he said. "Now I think we're brave enough for anything. I mean, you got up before dawn and cooked a feast for the fiercest judge on TV. Not to mention you've had four sleepovers in a row this past week."

"It's not so hard," she said. "The sleepovers, I mean. Cooking for Tom Truffleman is the worst."

He nodded, stealing a forkful of her cake. She allowed that too.

"I found a great quote once by a journalist named Harriet Van Horne," James said. "She said 'cooking is like love.' It should be entered into with abandon or not at all.'"

When you did something with abandon, Alice knew, you did it with your whole heart. She knew what it felt like to cook with abandon — you lost track of time and space, and your heart felt as light as puff pastry, as bright as a sparkler.

Maybe that was what love felt like too?

She decided not to ask — she didn't really need to know. She picked up her fork and, together with her father, finished off the cake.

Once the cake was gone, Alice left James on the terrace with the history of the potato ricer and went to find Tavi and Henry.

As she passed by the ballroom on the way to the lobby, she heard a commotion that made her pause. Inside, the serving staff was setting up tables and chairs for the feast. Richard was shouting instructions, reminding them not to scuff the floors. And in the far corner of the room, Hana Holmes was perusing the Victorian inventions and oddities.

Alice slipped inside and headed for the exhibit. "Cool scooter, hey?" she said, sidling up to Hana.

She nodded without taking her eyes off it. "Can you imagine Lady Norman scooting through the streets of London? Can you imagine the anger she faced every day, just because she was unaccompanied by a man? Also, I bet this was a rough ride."

Alice was about to say that it was surprisingly smooth and zippy when Hana spun toward her. "Oh my god, *Alice!* You're here! Is the competition over?"

She nodded, though she still couldn't believe it.

"How did it go?"

"Not the way I thought it would. But it's a long story. Can I tell you later?"

"Sure, I —"

"I'm sorry," Alice blurted. "For . . ." She gestured to Hana's bruise, which had taken on a greenish tinge. "You know."

"Oh, Alice." Hana smiled. "It's fine, honestly. When you take up Bartitsu as a hobby, you know you're going to get some bruises. It's risky business, Bartitsu."

Risky business — that was what James had said about love.

"And I want to apologize too." Hana went on.

"You do?"

Hana nodded. "For bringing us here. For signing you guys up for a competition that turned out to be complete torture."

"It wasn't *complete* torture —"

"This hasn't been a fun vacation for any of us," Hana said dejectedly. "I'm really looking forward to going home tomorrow. Aren't you?"

A few days before, Alice would have said yes, absolutely. But now she felt differently. Now she had work to do, a mystery to solve and friends to solve it with. She wouldn't have had any of those things if they'd escaped on the first day, as she'd wanted to.

"Not really," she began, but she didn't get a chance to explain, because, all of a sudden, a whippet burst into the ballroom.

"Roslyn!" Richard cried. "What are you doing?"

Roslyn ignored him, sprinting around the room with her tongue flapping in the breeze.

Hana shook her head. "That dog is so weird."

"Stop!" Richard bellowed, and finally the whippet obeyed. She sat down under the painting of the silver racehorse and whined.

"I'm so sorry, everyone." Richard hurried across the room and grabbed Roslyn by her collar. "Her dog walker is away and she isn't getting nearly enough exercise. Are you, sweetums? Come with me." Roslyn reluctantly followed him out the door.

"Weird," said Hana. Then she turned back to Alice. "Hey, have you ever heard of mochi ice cream?"

"What's that?"

"A Japanese dessert. I think you'll like it." Hana pulled out her phone and tapped open her PHOMO app. "Look." She held up a photo of a cluster of pastel-colored balls. One had been sliced open, revealing an ice cream center.

"Cool!" Alice exclaimed. "How do you make this?"

"To be honest, I'm not sure," said Hana. "But it's delicious — I ate so much on my last trip to Japan. That's where I took this photo — it's on my account if you want to see more. Anyway, I thought maybe we could try making it . . . sometime . . . together," she added hesitantly.

"Yes, please!" Alice grinned. "Maybe when we —" She stopped suddenly as another photo caught her eye. "Wait, what's that?"

"This?" Hana tapped open the latest photo posted on her account. It showed a sparkling, hourglass-shaped pool rimmed by white patio chairs topped with red-striped towels. "The spa down the road."

Alice stared at it. It looked oddly familiar.

"It's really lovely," said Hana. "I'm so glad the Sapphires suggested we go yesterday. You can even order poolside drinks with —"

"Wait, this is the *spa*?"

Hana nodded.

"The spa down the road," Alice said, just to be sure.

"Yes. Remember, I went there with Tavi's parents yesterday?"

"Oh my gosh." Alice's brain was revving like Lady Norman's scooter. "And you posted that on PHOMO."

"Uh-huh." Hana looked puzzled. "Do you want to stop there on the way home tomorrow?"

"No. I mean, maybe. I mean, I have to go," said Alice. She turned and hurried back to the door.

"Are you okay?" Hana called.

Alice waved over her shoulder, then began to run.

CHAPTER
23

They held an emergency meeting in the library — a door-closer if ever there was one.

"Look." Alice's hands were shaking as she tapped open her PHOMO app and searched for the photo. She held it up so Tavi and Henry could see.

"François's selfie from Belize?" said Henry. "What's suspicious about that?"

"Other than the terrible filter he used," added Tavi.

"That's not Belize," Alice told them. "He took that at the spa down the road."

"What?!" Tavi squawked.

She then found the photo Hana had shown her: the scene was identical, right down to the striped towels on the patio chairs.

"No way!" Henry's eyes widened. "He's pretending to be in Belize when he never even left the neighborhood?"

"That is *super* suspicious," said Tavi.

"Definitely." Henry grabbed his notebook and began scribbling furiously. "Let's search his account and see what else we can find."

"Looks like he goes by Frank," Alice noted as she read through his profile information. "I guess that's short for François?"

"Also known as Frank." Henry noted this. "Anything else?"

"He takes a lot of selfies," Tavi observed. "And those filters are doing nothing for him. He needs a lesson from Miranda Summers — now she knows how to use filters."

Alice scrolled through selfie after selfie: Frank eating breakfast, Frank working out at the gym, Frank hanging out with friends —

"Wait a second!" She looked more closely at a photo, then held it up for Tavi and Henry to see. "He's friends with Richard Sibley-McFinch!"

Henry dropped his pen. "You're kidding!"

The photo, posted the previous summer, showed Frank and Richard standing on the terrace at Gladstone Manor, raising their wine glasses to the camera. Frank's caption read: "Cheers to old friends!"

"Super-duper suspicious," muttered Tavi. "But what does it — Oh my gosh, look!"

Alice peeked over her shoulder. "It's Roslyn!"

Tavi turned her phone so that Henry could see the selfie Frank had taken with the whippet curled up in his lap. "A dog walker's work is never done," he'd written. "And I wouldn't have it any other way. I love this troublemaker!"

"He's the *dog walker*!" Alice recalled Richard saying, not half an hour earlier, that Roslyn's dog walker was out of town. Did he know Frank was staying at the spa down the road?

"Could Frank be our saboteur?" Tavi looked up from her phone.

Henry's eyes gleamed. "I'd say we have a new prime suspect."

"A PS," Tavi whispered, "on the DL."

"But why would he do it?" asked Alice. "Why would he be sabotaging the show that's being filmed at Richard's hotel?"

"Excellent question," said Henry. But he had no answers.

"Maybe we could go to the spa to investigate?" Tavi suggested. "I could ask my parents if they'd drive us, although they probably want to be here for the feast. They've spent hours prepping their costumes."

"And it starts in half an hour," Henry pointed out.

"Also," said Alice, "he might still be around." She told them about the green slime that had appeared on her pie filling that afternoon. "Maybe he's long gone by now —"

"Or maybe he's in our midst," Henry finished. "I wonder where."

Tavi turned back to Frank's photos. "If only Roslyn could show us. I bet she knows where he is."

Henry hummed and looked back at his notes.

"Roslyn . . ." Alice murmured.

"I mean, she's obviously not talking or anything, but —"

"Unless . . ." Alice straightened as a new thought came to mind. "Unless she is?"

"Sorry?"

Henry looked up from his notes. "Say more."

She leaned forward. "Here's what I'm thinking."

They waited until the feast began before putting their hastily made plan into action. Alice told her father she'd be a bit late but promised she'd be there soon. When he asked why, she made up a quick excuse.

"I'm . . . making a gift."

"A gift? For whom?"

"Um . . . Hana?"

He looked deeply skeptical, and she felt a bit guilty for lying. She dashed off before he could ask more questions.

She met Tavi and Henry at the Great Hall, which was both unlocked and empty, just as they'd hoped. The cameras and lights had been moved to the ballroom — all that was left were three workstations, which Alice guessed would be dismantled the following day. She took a moment to say goodbye to her Superchef stand mixer, then got to work.

"Which one was it?" asked Tavi.

"This one." She led them over to the painting that Roslyn had stopped and howled at — the painting of the old man who looked a bit like Tom Truffleman. He glared down at them as they inspected the enormous framed canvas. It was easily as tall as Alice and probably twice as heavy.

"How could he have taken it down?" Tavi wondered.

"He didn't have to," said Henry. "Look!" He pointed to the right side of the frame, where a set of hinges connected it to the wall. "This is brilliant!" He darted over to the left side of the painting, grabbed the frame and swung it open like a door. Behind it was a real door: old, wooden and open just a crack.

"Whoa," said Tavi.

Henry pushed the door open, revealing a dark hallway.

"A secret passage!" cried Alice.

"The game is afoot!" declared Henry. He pulled out his phone and switched on the flashlight. "Let's follow it."

Alice and Tavi took out their phones, switched on their flashlights and followed him in. The passage was small — Alice could touch both walls if she spread her arms, and Tavi's head nearly brushed the ceiling. The wood underfoot felt spongy and uneven, and every now and then it let out a creak that made Alice's heart stutter. She'd forgotten how much she disliked small, dark spaces. Especially small, dark spaces possibly inhabited by criminals.

She forced herself to take deep breaths and keep moving.

Henry stopped suddenly, and Alice bumped into his back, nearly dropping her phone.

"What is it?" asked Tavi.

"A room." He shone his flashlight to the right, revealing an opening in the wall and a room beyond it, about the size of Alice's bedroom at home. "I wonder if it was once a servant's room? This passage might lead to the kitchen or something."

Alice shone her light around the space and found a toolbox in one corner. Beside it stood what looked like a trash can.

"The saboteur's lair," Tavi hissed. Alice shivered.

"He even has a wireless charging station for his phone!" Henry stepped into the room and pointed his flashlight at a dock near the wall. "This is the perfect hiding place," he marveled. "He has easy access to the Great Hall and who knows how many other rooms!"

Alice walked over to the trash and knelt to inspect it. Along with at least a dozen candy bar wrappers, she found a half-full bottle of olive oil and an empty box of green Jell-o.

"No way," she breathed. Then she noticed something tucked behind the trash can. A piece of cloth, frayed at the edges.

Her father's lucky scarf.

She grabbed it off the cold floor and wrapped it around her neck. "You guys!" she whispered. "Come look! There's a box of green Jell-o, a bottle of olive oil and, oh my gosh, there are salt and sugar labels too! And —"

A creak from the passage made them all freeze.

"Lights off!" Henry commanded.

They fumbled for their phones, but before they could switch them off, a man-sized figure appeared in the doorway and shone a flashlight around the room.

The saboteur froze. They held their breath.

Then he turned on his heel and ran back the way he'd come.

"Get him!" Henry cried.

They charged back out into the passage, following the saboteur's flashlight.

"To the right!" Tavi called as the light disappeared. "There's another passage to the right!" They turned right and saw the light again, then heard the man stumble and swear.

"Hurry!" Henry picked up the pace. "I think it's a dead end! We've got him cornered!"

In the light from Henry's phone, Alice saw the man stop and look back. For the first time, she saw his face clearly: it was François, or Frank. And he was not pleased. She briefly wondered what they were going to do when they caught up to him, and whether it was really a good idea to corner a criminal in a secret passage, and whether they should have thought this through before charging after him.

"We've got him!" yelled Henry.

"Oh no you don't!" Frank grunted. Suddenly the passage was flooded with light, and he disappeared into it. Then came a crash and the sound of breaking glass, followed by a scream.

Alice tried to stop, but Tavi pushed her on, and soon they too were hurtling into the light and tripping over Henry, who was lying on the floor. They landed in a heap beside him and Frank.

It took Alice a moment to realize that they'd crashed through another door behind another painting. They were in the middle of the ballroom.

"What's going on?" someone shrieked.

"Is that Alice?"

"Is that *François*?"

Frank hopped to his feet and ran on.

"Stop him!" Henry hollered. "He's a saboteur!"

"Alice!" someone yelled, and she knew it was her father, but she couldn't stop to look. She untangled her limbs from Tavi's and ran after Henry, who was running after Frank, who was heading for the ballroom door. Guests shrieked as they passed. A man fell out of his chair. A server dropped a bowl of soup on the floor.

"Is this the entertainment?" a guest wondered as Alice ran past.

"A bit much, isn't it?" said another.

"Help us!" Alice called to them as she hurdled the spilled soup. "He sabotaged *Culinary Combat!*"

Now Frank was nearing the door. Henry grabbed a loaf of bread off a table and launched it at his back, catching him between the shoulders. But Frank kept going.

Alice was about to holler for help again — why wouldn't the adults do something? — when she heard a buzzing noise, growing louder. She looked back to see Tavi roaring toward her on Lady Norman's scooter.

"Yes!" she screamed, but she was drowned out by the rumble of the motor and the shrieks of the guests.

"That's an antique!" someone screeched.

"Come on!" Tavi slowed so Alice could hop on behind her. They zipped across the room, cutting Frank off just before he reached the door.

Frank stumbled backward in surprise. "Get away from me, you stupid kids," he snarled.

Tavi cut the motor, and they hopped off the scooter to face him.

"You sabotaged the whole competition!" Alice yelled, loudly enough for everyone to hear. "We know about everything you did!"

"You took the labels off the sugar and salt!" cried Tavi.

"You stole my dad's scarf!"

"You poured olive oil on Phyllis's oven mitts."

"And you ruined my peacock pie!"

Frank paled. "Get away from me," he repeated, then he turned and lunged for the door. But instead, he pitched forward, landing smack on his chest on the floor. Again, the guests shrieked.

"What the —" Alice looked up to see Henry holding a cane, the crook of which was hooked around Frank's ankle. It was the cane from the exhibit — the one that turned into an umbrella, a flute and a butterfly net. With one swift, practiced motion, he'd taken down the saboteur.

"Next-level Bartitsu," he said smugly.

"**W**hat on earth is going on?" James came running toward them, windmilling his arms.

Hana was hot on his heels. "Did you say he's a saboteur?" she demanded. Before Alice could explain, she was on the floor, pinning Frank's shoulders to the ground.

"Ladies and gentlemen!" Henry turned to face the room. "I'm Detective Oh, and these are my colleagues, Detective Fleck and Detective Sapphire. We're sorry to interrupt your dinner, but frankly this is more important. This man," he pointed at Frank, "is a criminal! He sabotaged the entire cooking competition, every single challenge!"

Now everyone was on their feet, jostling for a better look. James gaped. "Alice, is this a joke?"

"This is no joke, Mr. Fleck," said Henry. "We have all kinds of evidence. But we don't yet know why he did it. So for the answer, we turn to . . ." He scanned the room. "Richard Sibley-McFinch!"

Everyone spun to face the manor owner, who was standing near the spilled soup, mouth wide open.

"Frank!" Richard stepped forward. "What's going on? I thought you were in Belize!"

Alice looked at Henry. Either Richard was a very good actor or he actually didn't know what was going on.

"What happened to the plane ticket I bought you?"

"You bought him a plane ticket?" said Tavi. "Why?"

On the floor, Frank groaned.

"Interesting." Henry tapped his chin. "Well, first, we should call the police. Mr. Sapphire, can you do that?"

Tavi's father hesitated. "Police? Really?"

"I think they'll want to know," said Tavi. Her father nodded and hurried away.

"And in the meantime," Henry continued, "let's see if we can piece this mystery together. Do you want to start, Alice?"

She took a deep breath. "After François got kicked off the show," she began, "he didn't go to Belize like he said. We know this because he posted photos on PHOMO from the spa down the road." She nodded at Hana, whose eyes widened.

"PHOMO also taught us that François, also known as Frank, is a good friend of Richard's — and Roslyn's," Tavi continued. "Alice noticed that the dog kept hanging around a few specific paintings in the Great Hall and the ballroom. On closer inspection, we found a secret passage connecting them. See for yourselves!" She pointed at the painting of the silver racehorse, which had swung wide open on its hinges when they made their big entrance.

"If you follow that passage," Henry went on, "you'll find a room with evidence from every *Culinary Combat* challenge that Frank sabotaged. We found the oil he poured over Phyllis's oven mitts, which made her drop her pigeon pie. And we found the labels he pulled off the jars of sugar and salt, which explains why Diana mixed up her ingredients."

"We also found this!" Alice took off her father's lucky scarf and handed it to him.

"My scarf!" cried James.

"You criminal!" Tom Truffleman roared, storming across the room. "You felon! How dare you mess with my show!" His fists were clenched, as though he wanted to pummel the saboteur, and he might have done just that had the production crew not held him back.

"I just don't know what to say." Richard's mustache drooped. "Frank, how could you?"

Frank didn't reply.

"Frank is my friend," he told the crowd. "I've known him for ages. Actually, he was the one who convinced me to host the show."

"Stop talking," Frank groaned from the floor. Hana silenced him with an elbow between his shoulder blades.

"A few months ago, he told me he'd always dreamed of competing on a cooking show," Richard went on. "I had no idea. I wanted to help him, so I worked with him on his audition video, and he was accepted to compete. We decided it was best if we didn't mention our friendship — we didn't want anyone thinking he'd been accepted unfairly." He looked down at Frank and scratched his head. "Honestly, I don't understand this at all."

"Let me up," Frank grunted. Hana allowed him to sit up but kept a hand on his shoulder in case he tried to flee.

"You owe us an explanation," Richard told him.

"Fine!" Frank spat. "I'll tell you why I did it. It's all *his* fault!" He pointed across the room. Once again everyone turned to look.

"*My* fault?" Tom Truffleman cried.

"Truffleman's fault?" said Henry.

"Look at me, Truffleman!" Frank yelled. Then he shook his head. "You really don't recognize me at all, do you?"

"Of course I recognize you." The judge looked irritated. "Six days ago, you tried to feed me raw cake batter."

"Not from this show!" Frank huffed. "I'm Franklin! Franklin Phibbs!"

Tom Truffleman looked blank.

"From *Kids Can Cook (Or Can They Really?)*!"

The judge shuddered. "Ugh, I hated that show."

"And you ruined my life because of it!" Frank thumped the floor with his fist. "You broke me, Tom Truffleman!"

"Wait, you were on his first cooking show?" Alice couldn't believe it.

Frank nodded. "Truffleman told me I would never be a chef, all because I flubbed a flambé and set a hand towel on fire. He made me cry on national TV, and the kids at my school never let me forget it! For months, they pretended to cry whenever they saw me. I had to change schools because of that."

Tom Truffleman took off his glasses and gave Frank a long look. Then he set them back on his nose. "Yeah, I don't remember that."

"Of course you don't!" Frank hollered. "That's just like you!"

"Okay, settle down," said Hana.

"So let me get this straight," said Alice. "You sabotaged everything to get revenge? Even my dad's stove, so he'd need to use Samir's?"

"I didn't know he'd do that," muttered Frank. "But yeah, I messed with the switches."

James shook his head. "I can't believe this."

"Me neither. It is so, so good," someone whispered behind Alice. She turned to see Meg with her video camera, filming Frank's confession.

She couldn't have planned it better herself.

The police arrived shortly after that. They seemed a bit uncertain about whether reality TV sabotage really warranted an investigation, but Tom Truffleman insisted, so they agreed to stay. One after another, people were called to the parlor to tell their stories: first Frank, then Tom Truffleman, then Richard, Jasmina, Meg, James, Sven and Samir, Toni and Tina and even Tavi's parents.

After what felt like an eternity, it was Alice, Henry and Tavi's turn. Their interview took longer than anyone else's, partly because they had so much to say and partly because Henry wanted to ask the inspectors how they'd gotten into their line of work, and whether they'd consider hiring him on contract, as his rates were very fair. They told him they'd keep him in mind.

Three hours later, the police gathered everyone in the parlor to recount the story they'd pieced together.

Nearly two decades after Franklin Phibbs had been publicly shamed by Tom Truffleman on *Kids Can Cook (Or Can They Really?)*, he was visiting his friend and employer, Richard Sibley-McFinch, and learned that a producer for *Culinary Chronicles* had recently contacted Richard, hoping to film the show at Gladstone Manor.

After all that time, Frank still secretly dreamed of cooking competitively, and he wondered if this might be his chance to ease back into it. After all, *Culinary Chronicles* was the friendliest cooking competition on TV, and practically no one watched it.

He encouraged Richard to host the show at Gladstone Manor, and he applied to be a contestant under the name François, which he'd always thought suited him better than Frank.

He'd already been accepted to compete when Richard shared some top-secret news: Frank would actually be competing on *Culinary Combat*, a RealiTV show featuring the very judge who'd dashed ten-year-old Frank's dreams.

And just like that, Frank changed his plans. Over the years he had thought up countless ways to take revenge on Tom Truffleman. Now he only had to pick one. Or two. Or seven.

"But he never did take revenge on Tom Truffleman," Alice interjected. "He only hurt the other contestants. Why would he do that?"

The inspectors explained that Frank felt every act of sabotage put him more in control of the show and took power away from Tom Truffleman.

"Maybe that's because Truffleman made him feel so helpless as a child," Mr. Sapphire suggested. "Now Frank craves control because back then he had so little."

And, the inspectors went on, Frank's greatest act of sabotage had yet to come. He had an entire flock of pigeons caged and waiting in the stables — he'd planned to release them at the feast, just as the famous judge announced the winner of *Culinary Combat*.

Alice recalled the video Samir had described, in which Tom Truffleman shrieked in terror at the sight of a single pigeon. He probably would have lost his mind.

"So what happens to Frank now?" asked Henry.

The police explained that the RealiTV lawyers would decide whether they wanted to press charges against him.

"He's definitely lost his dog-walking job," Richard added. And judging by the grim look on his face, Frank had lost his friend as well.

Although she deeply resented him for sabotaging the competition, Alice couldn't help but feel sad for Frank. "He spent *twenty years* plotting revenge on Tom Truffleman," she marveled to Tavi and Henry. "That's a crazy long time."

"They say revenge is a dish best served cold," said Henry. When Alice raised her eyebrows, he explained, "That means revenge is more satisfying when it happens a long time after the original crime." He shrugged. "I don't know why."

"A dish best served cold," she repeated. Given the situation, it was the perfect phrase.

"And speaking of dishes served cold..." Tavi nodded toward Hana, who'd just arrived carrying plates of food the serving staff had set aside for them. There was no peacock pie left (to Alice's relief), but they helped themselves to duchess potatoes, stuffed eggplant and thick slices of fresh bread.

It was nearly midnight by the time they all returned to the ballroom, but the guests were all still there, bright-eyed, full-bellied and eager to find out who'd won the competition. They rearranged their seats so Alice, Tavi and Henry, plus James, Hana and Tavi's parents, could sit at a table beside the other contestants.

Tavi and Henry linked their arms through Alice's as Tom Truffleman and Miranda Summers stood to declare the winner.

"First off," Miranda began, "let's thank our competitors for the delicious feast they made us." She paused for applause. "As you can imagine, it's hard to name a winner knowing there has been a saboteur on set. And the producers have decided that the contestants who left us will be invited back next season to try again. Except Frank, of course."

Alice raised her eyebrows at her father. Would he want to try again?

"Not on your life," he said.

She smiled, relieved.

"But we can't have a competition without a winner," said Tom Truffleman. "And so it's my pleasure to announce that the winners of the first season of *Culinary Combat* are . . ." He paused. "Sven and Samir."

The crowd erupted into cheers, and Alice cheered loudest of all. It only made sense: Sven and Samir were excellent cooks. They deserved to win.

"Toni and Tina did very well too," Miranda prompted Tom.

He nodded. "Good bread. Decent dessert. Your peacock pie was as tough as leather but, well, that's peacock."

Toni and Tina hugged, and Alice heard Toni whisper, "Let's never do this again."

"And Alice . . ." said Miranda.

"And Alice." Tom Truffleman looked around until he found her in the crowd. "Alice . . . didn't make all the dishes I asked for."

"Because Frank sabotaged her pie!" shouted Toni.

"True," he allowed. "But Alice made something different. Something unique. Something . . . special." He waved, and Jasmina appeared with the telephone sculpture and a sharp chef's knife. While everyone watched, Truffleman sliced through the rotary dial, revealing perfect layers of chocolate cake. The guests oohed and aahed. "This is anything but boring," he proclaimed. "In fact, I'd say it's a work of art."

Alice gasped. A work of *art*?

"You know, Tom, I think you learned something from this," said Miranda.

He pursed his lips, then nodded. "I suppose I've learned that . . . well, some kids really can cook. Not all of them!" he added hastily. "But a few."

The crowd cheered. Tavi and Henry threw their arms around Alice, whose face hurt from smiling so broadly.

"A toast to the all chefs!" Miranda grabbed a glass of champagne.

"To the chefs!" The guests rose to their feet and raised their glasses.

"But especially to Alice!" the twins added.

"To Alice," James agreed, raising his glass to her. "The bravest and best sous-chef . . . I mean, the bravest and best *chef* I know."

Feeling as light as puff pastry and as bright as a sparkler, Alice took her glass of lemonade and raised it in the air. "To all of us!" she declared.

CHAPTER 25

TWO MONTHS LATER

On her very first day of middle school, Alice Fleck came downstairs to find an unexpected gift.

"Open it!" Her father pressed a rectangular box into her hands. He was still dressed in his bathrobe and slippers, bed-headed as usual.

Alice lifted the lid and gasped. "You're kidding!"

He nodded excitedly. "It's a thermometer, propane torch, heat gun and hand blender, all in one tool! Isn't that incredible? It looks like something the Victorians would have invented."

"Wow!" She lifted the multi-tool out of the box, picturing the crème brûlée she'd torch and the chocolate she'd temper. "Thank you so much!"

"It's a good-luck gift for your first day of seventh grade!" He beamed. "Secondhand, of course — I found it at a garage sale. But it's in great condition."

"I love it," she told him, and she gave him a big hug.

"Now, are you ready? Where's your lunch?"

"In the fridge where I left it," she said. "I won't forget."

According to Mat, they could actually buy lunch at their new school, but Alice had decided to bring her own and fill it with food she'd made herself, like the stuffed eggplant she'd perfected over the summer and Samir's favorite halva, which was just as delicious as he'd said.

Her phone buzzed in her pocket, and she pulled it out to find a text from Hana: Good luck today, Alice! See you tonight for dinner!

Alice sent back a thumbs-up emoji. Hana joined them for at least two dinners a week now, as well as regular cooking sessions. They'd made many batches of mochi ice cream over the summer and had plans to try a beautiful Japanese confection called *dango*, which conveniently had its own emoji. Alice added one of those to her message back to Hana, along with a heart.

James emerged from the kitchen with her lunch just as the phone buzzed again. This time it was Henry.

Good luck today! Don't forget to look for mysteries.

Alice grinned. She, Henry and Tavi still got together at least once a week to recount their adventures at Gladstone Manor, watch *Desserts to Die For* and make plans for the detective agency that Henry had insisted they launch. They called themselves The Down-Low Detectives, and they were available for hire on evenings and weekends. When Mat had returned from art camp, Alice had introduced him to her new friends, and he'd immediately offered to make them a logo for the agency, using the graphic design skills he'd picked up.

She was just tucking the phone into her backpack when it buzzed a third time. Her father shook his head and muttered something about kaleidoscopes as he handed over her lunch bag.

It was a message from Tavi: I'm waiting for the bus and look what's here! It's almost like you're with me.

Alice tapped open the photo she'd attached. It showed a bus shelter poster featuring Alice herself. She was wearing her apron and piping ladyfingers onto a cookie sheet, her eyes narrowed in concentration. Below her, in big block letters, the poster read: CULINARY COMBAT: SEASON 1. THE BATTLE BEGINS ON SEPTEMBER 15.

She shivered. She'd seen the show posters before — in a shopping mall, on the side of a bus, even in an ad on PHOMO — but the sight still gave her goosebumps. She knew she'd never get used to being the face of *Culinary Combat.*

Can't wait for the party! Tavi added, along with a string of heart and star emojis.

Despite her mixed feelings about the show itself, Alice was also looking forward to their viewing party. She and her father had invited friends and family and lots of people from the show to watch the first episode together at their townhouse. There would be food, of course, and since the Sapphires were coming there would probably be costumes too.

Alice couldn't wait to catch up with the other contestants, whom she hadn't seen in nearly a month. Everyone had been so busy. Sven and Samir were hard at work on their cookbook, and Toni and Tina were planning to open their very own churro shop, called Abuelita's. Diana, meanwhile, was starting university — her goal was to become an emergency room doctor. She'd be attending the school where Phyllis taught courses in culinary history.

James and Alice had invited the production crew to the party too, and Jasmina had promised to drop by. She'd quit *Culinary Combat* the day after the feast and had taken the summer off to rethink her career. Last they'd heard, she was planning to pitch her very own show, *Two Many Cooks,* to the RealiTV executives.

In it, strangers would find love — or find they couldn't stand each other — when paired up to cook in very small kitchens. Miranda Summers had agreed to host if the executives gave the go-ahead.

They'd even invited Tom Truffleman to the party, but he'd said he was far too busy. He was already working on the next season of *Culinary Combat*, which he claimed would be bigger and better than ever. It would take place at an amusement park, and the contestants would have to cook while riding a roller coaster.

"You're sure you haven't forgotten anything?" James asked as Alice opened the front door. She could see Mat waiting on the sidewalk, his backpack bulging with supplies for his locker diorama. The day before, she'd helped him draw up plans for an amazing underwater scene.

"Dad, stop worrying!"

"I'm not worrying!" he protested, then added, "Much. I'm not worrying much."

"You're going to make *me* worried!" Alice told him.

"Sorry, sorry. All right." He dropped a kiss on her forehead. "You've got everything you need?"

She took stock of everything she had with her: notebooks and pens, a lunch made with love, a phone full of messages from people who cared. She had everything she needed to survive middle school. "I've got this," she said.

"You absolutely do," he agreed.

She smiled, then marched out the door.

AUTHOR'S NOTE

There are few things I love more than doing research for a novel — you never know where it will take you. For *Alice Fleck's Recipes for Disaster*, I went down many a rabbit hole, discovering fascinating facts about culinary history, Victorian inventions and cooking competitions. I tried my best to represent them accurately in this book. I also had fun watching many, many competitive cooking shows, but unlike the historical facts, *Culinary Combat* is entirely made up. If you're curious to know more about things you encountered in this book, from peacock pie to pteridomania to Bartitsu, you can visit my website, rachelledelaney.com, where you'll find articles, books and podcasts to explore.

ACKNOWLEDGMENTS

Enormous thanks to everyone who contributed to this novel — as always, the list is long. Amy Tompkins championed Alice from the very beginning. Lynne Missen continued to be the most supportive, insightful and lovely editor an author could hope for. Jude Somers generously answered my many questions about her time as a competitor on *The Great Canadian Baking Show* (many thanks to Shanna Baker for connecting us). Vikki Vansickle, Eric Simons, Louise Delaney, Stacey Matson, Tanya Kyi and the Inkslingers read early drafts of the novel and offered astute advice. Eric also braved Bartitsu class and watched innumerable competitive cooking shows with me. Catherine Majoribanks made everything better with her excellent copy-edit. Illustrator Morgan Goble created the wonderful cover art and Emma Dolan did a beautiful job on the book design. And the entire team at Penguin Random House Canada was fabulous to work with, as always.

Thank you all!